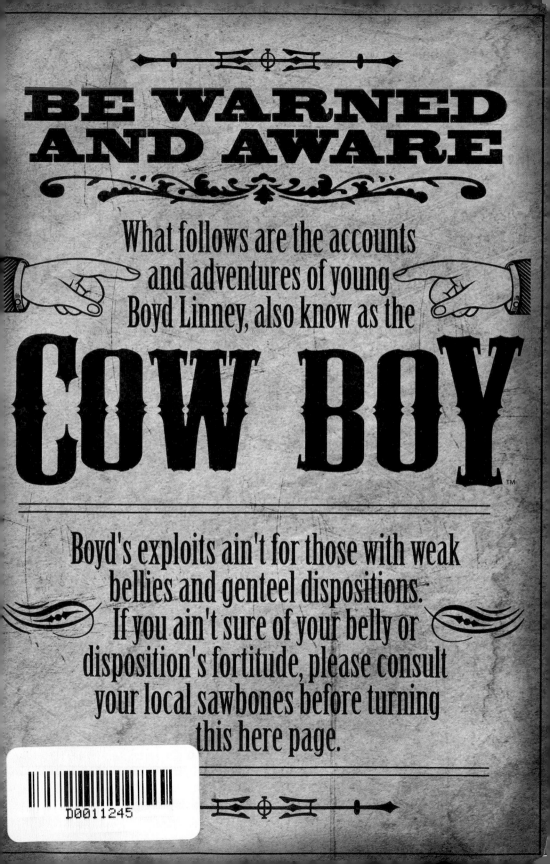

BE WARNED AND AWARE

What follows are the accounts
and adventures of young
Boyd Linney, also know as the

COW BOY

™

Boyd's exploits ain't for those with weak
bellies and genteel dispositions.
If you ain't sure of your belly or
disposition's fortitude, please consult
your local sawbones before turning
this here page.

COW BOY: A BOY

has been brought to y'all

Fella what goes by Mister

NATE COSBY

came up with the script  story, then

COW BOY'S

comprised of five chapters, broken up by brand-new yarns, courtesy of

Mister **ROGER LANGRIDGE**

Mister **BRIAN CLEVINGER**,
Mister **SCOTT WEGENER**, Mister **MITCH GERADS**

Ms. **COLLEEN COOVER**

Mister **MIKE MAIHACK.**

COW BOY was created by Mister Nate Cosby and Mister Chris Eliopoulos, but it would not have been possible without the aid of
Mister **CLAYTON COWLES.**

AND HIS HORSE ™

by these fine folk...

Mister

CHRIS ELIOPOULOS

came along and drew, colored  lettered it.

This here book's been published by the fine folks at Archaia, a division of Boom Entertainment, Inc.

Mister PAUL MORRISSEY is the fine editor of the original edition

and for this here softcover edition,

Ms. WHITNEY LEOPARD is the Associate Editor

and Ms. REBECCA TAYLOR is our Editor

ARCHAIA ™

ROSS RICHIE CEO & Founder
MARK SMYLIE Founder of Archaia
MATT GAGNON Editor-in-Chief
FILIP SABLIK President of Publishing & Marketing
STEPHEN CHRISTY President of Development
LANCE KREITER VP of Licensing & Merchandising
PHIL BARBARO VP of Finance
BRYCE CARLSON Managing Editor

MEL CAYLO Marketing Manager
SCOTT NEWMAN Production Design Manager
IRENE BRADISH Operations Manager
CHRISTINE DINH Brand Communications Manager
DAFNA PLEBAN Editor
SHANNON WATTERS Editor
ERIC HARBURN Editor
REBECCA TAYLOR Editor

IAN BRILL Editor
WHITNEY LEOPARD Associate Editor
JASMINE AMIRI Associate Editor
CHRIS ROSA Assistant Editor
ALEX GALER Assistant Editor
CAMERON CHITTOCK Assistant Editor
MARY GUMPORT Assistant Editor
KELSEY DIETERICH Production Designer

JILLIAN CRAB Production Designer
KARA LEOPARD Production Designer
DEVIN FUNCHES E-Commerce & Inventory Coordinator
AARON FERRARA Operations Coordinator
JOSÉ MEZA Sales Assistant
MICHELLE ANKLEY Sales Assistant
ELIZABETH LOUGHRIDGE Accounting Assistant
STEPHANIE HOCUTT PR Assistant

BOOM! Studios, 5670 Wilshire Boulevard, Suite 450, Los Angeles, CA 90036-5679. Printed in Korea. First Printing.
ISBN: 978-1-60886-419-5, eISBN: 978-1-61398-273-0

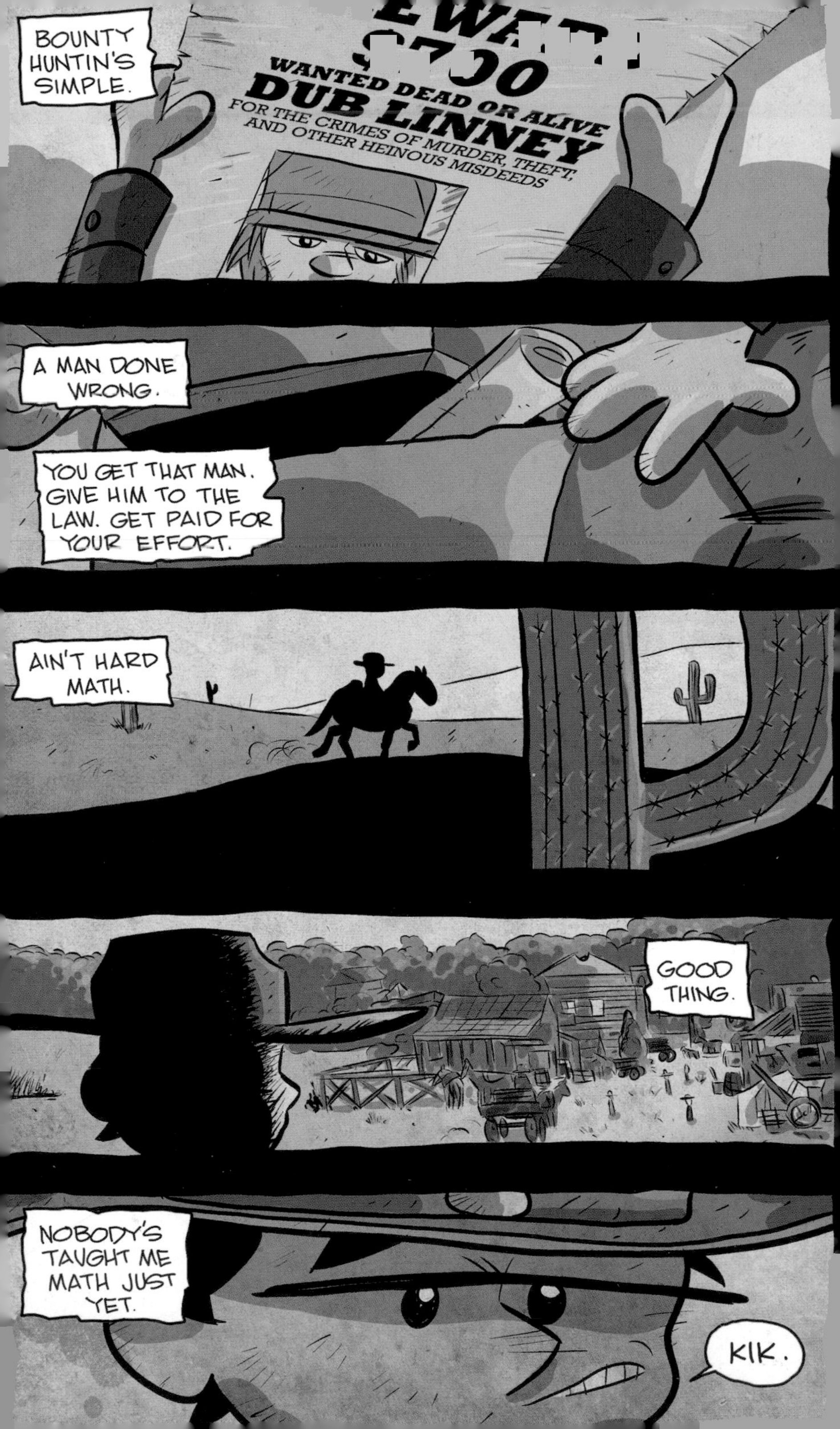
BOUNTY HUNTIN'S SIMPLE.
WANTED DEAD OR ALIVE
DUB LINNEY
FOR THE CRIMES OF MURDER, THEFT, AND OTHER HEINOUS MISDEEDS
A MAN DONE WRONG.
YOU GET THAT MAN. GIVE HIM TO THE LAW. GET PAID FOR YOUR EFFORT.
AIN'T HARD MATH.
GOOD THING.
NOBODY'S TAUGHT ME MATH JUST YET.
KIK.

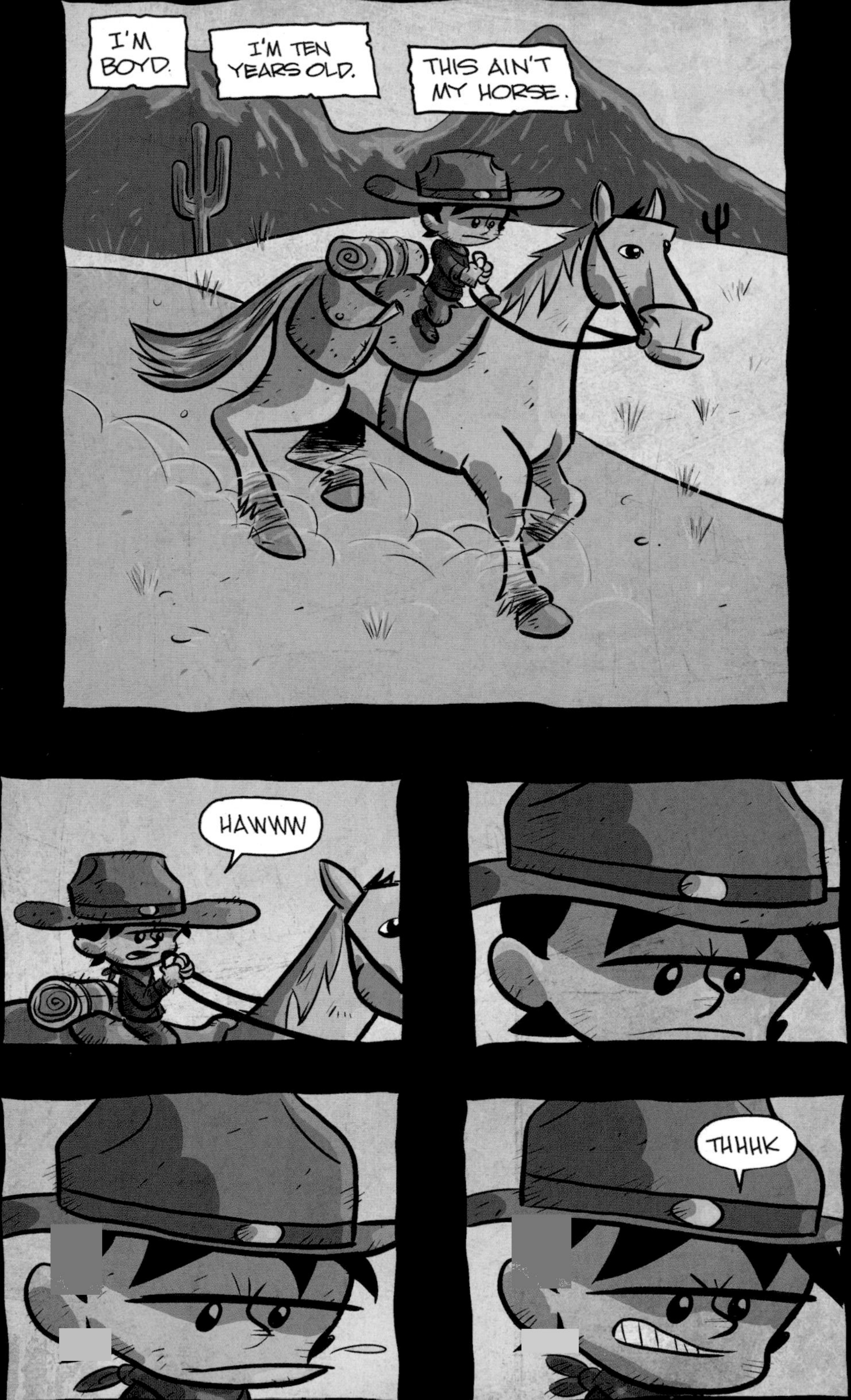
I'M BOYD.
I'M TEN YEARS OLD.
THIS AIN'T MY HORSE.
HAWWW
THHHK

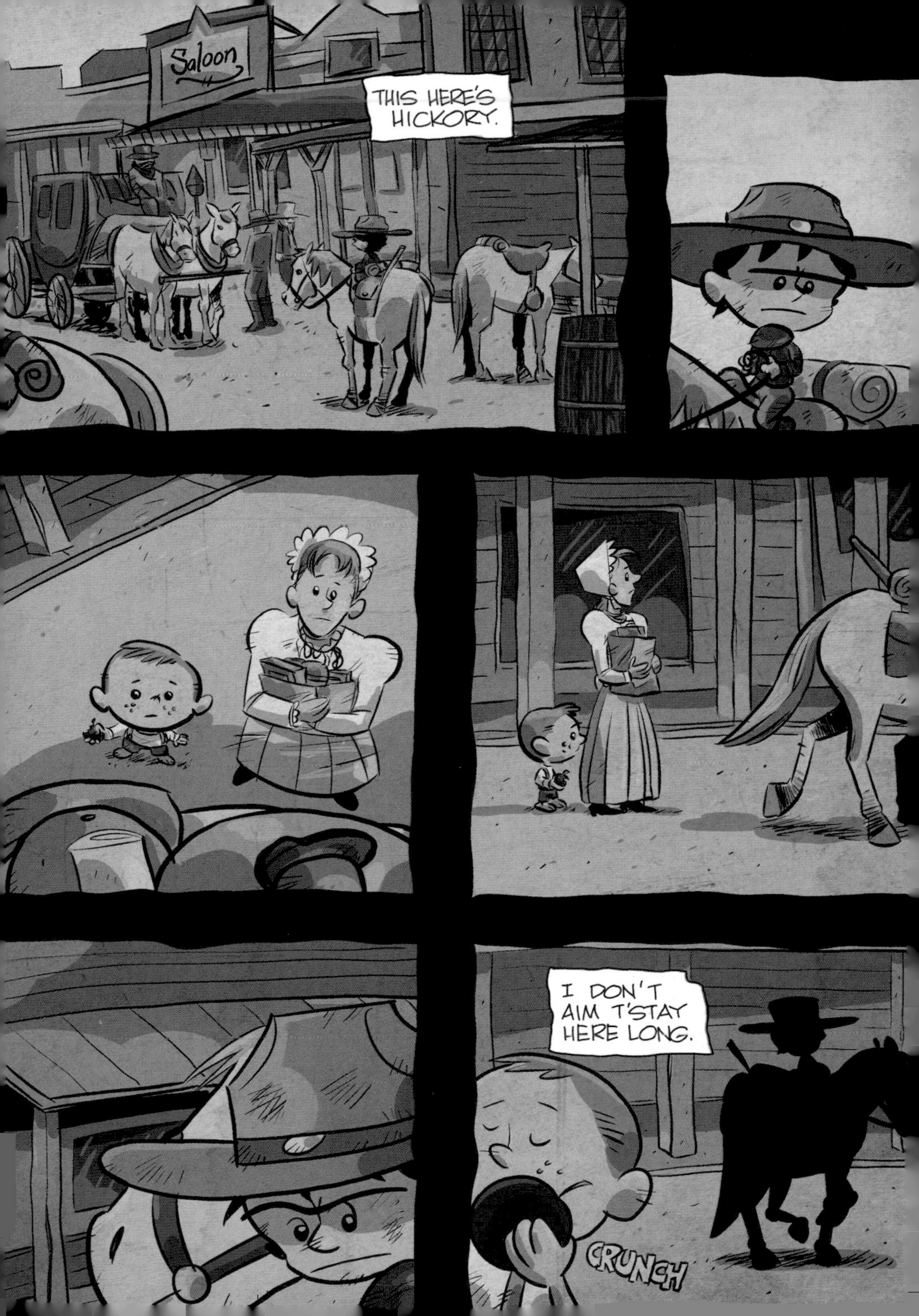
Saloon
THIS HERE'S HICKORY.
I DON'T AIM T'STAY HERE LONG.
CRUNCH

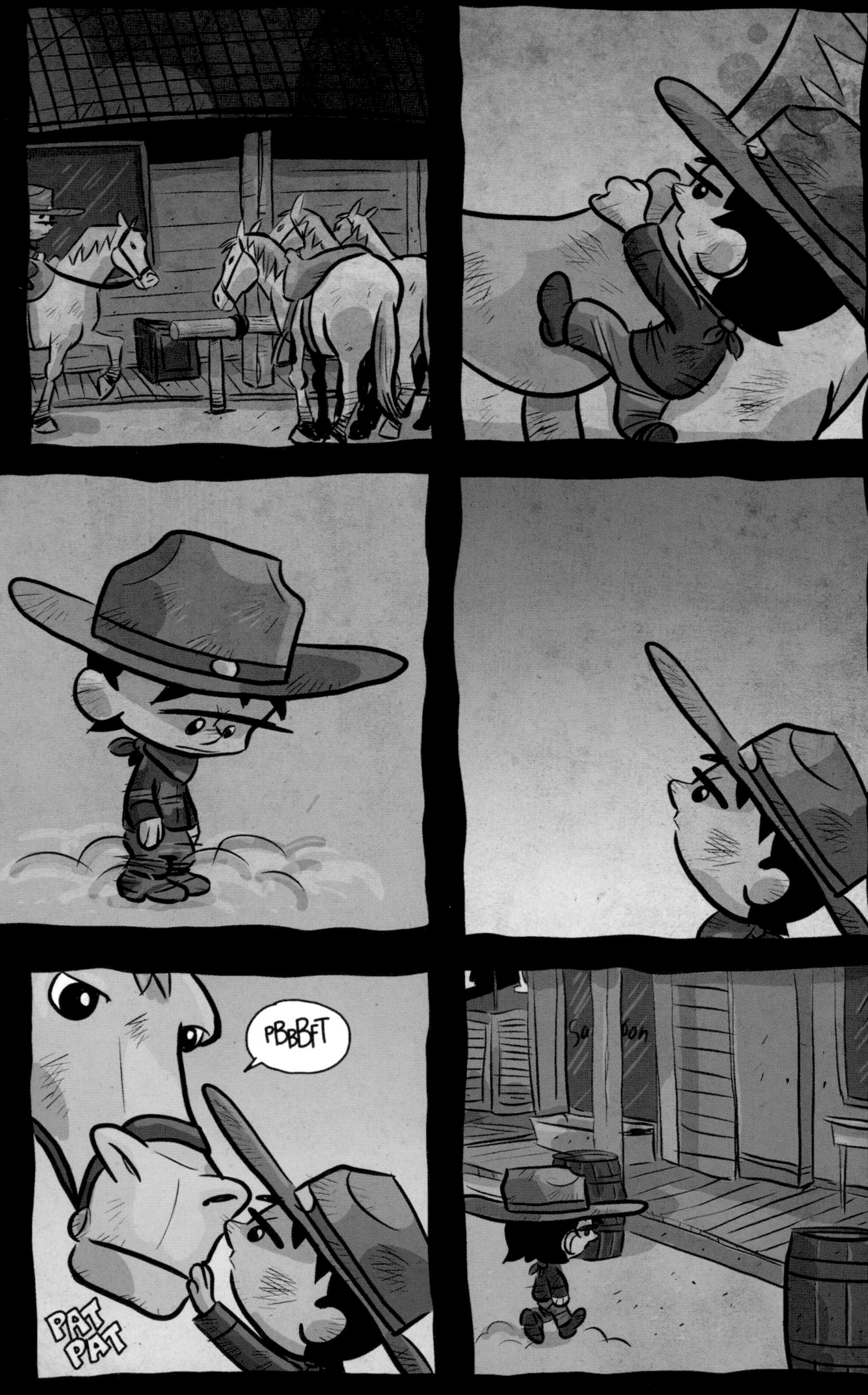
PBBBFT
PAT PAT

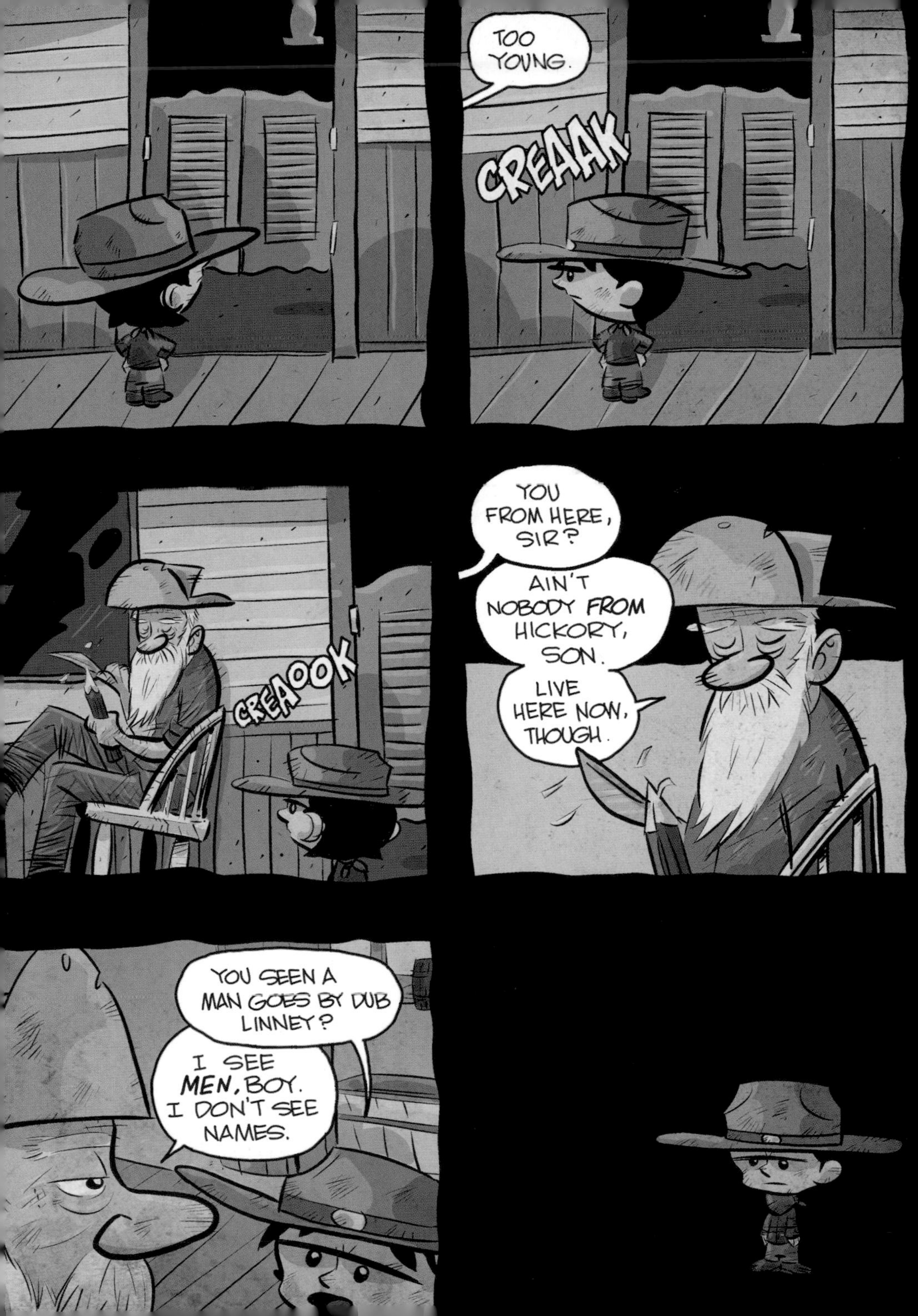
TOO YOUNG.
CREAAK
CREAOOK
YOU FROM HERE, SIR?
AIN'T NOBODY FROM HICKORY, SON.
LIVE HERE NOW, THOUGH.
YOU SEEN A MAN GOES BY DUB LINNEY?
I SEE MEN, BOY. I DON'T SEE NAMES.

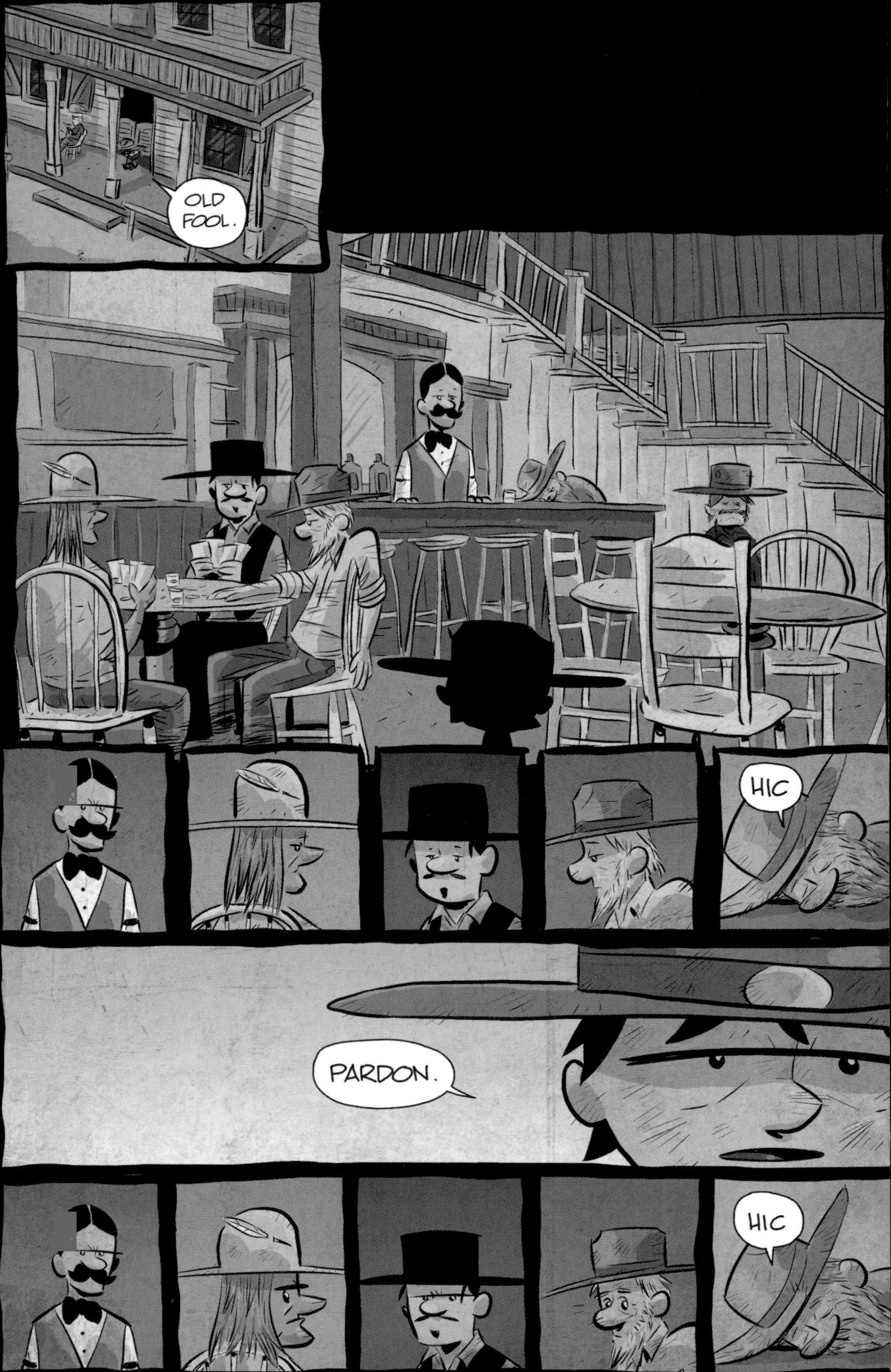
OLD FOOL.
HIC
PARDON.
HIC

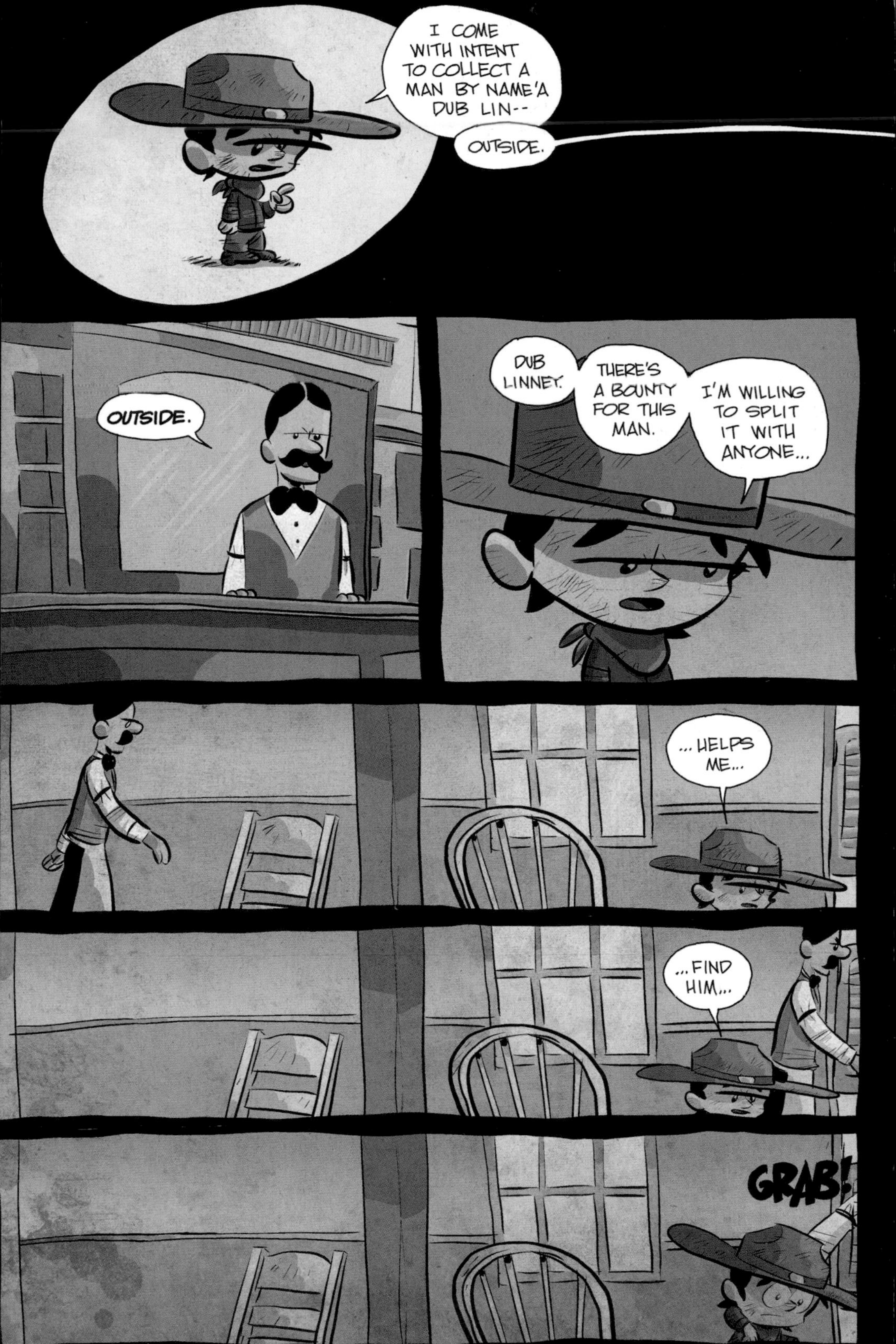
I COME WITH INTENT TO COLLECT A MAN BY NAME'A DUB LIN--
OUTSIDE.
OUTSIDE.
DUB LINNEY.
THERE'S A BOUNTY FOR THIS MAN.
I'M WILLING TO SPLIT IT WITH ANYONE...
...HELPS ME...
...FIND HIM...
GRAB!

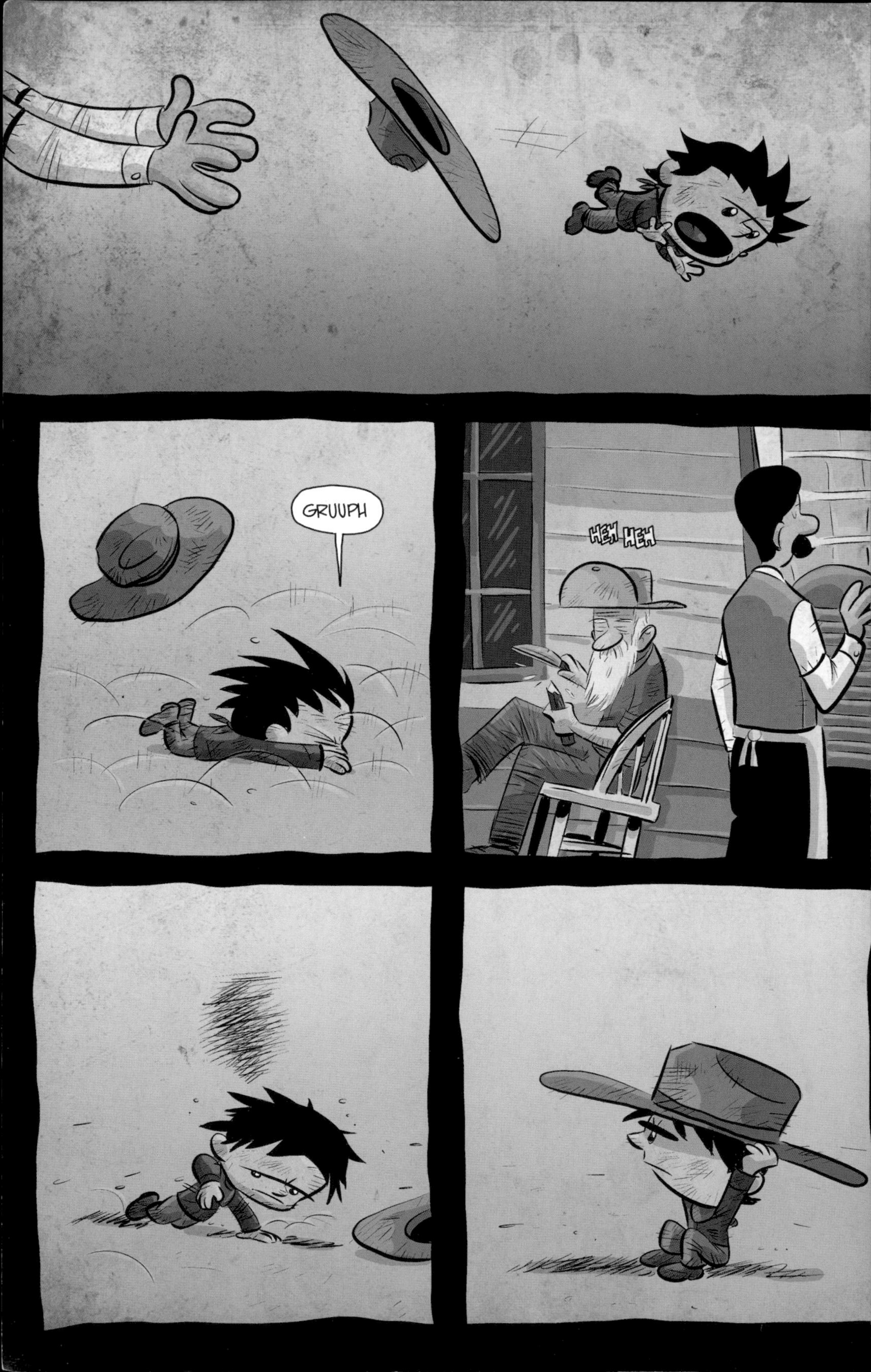
GRUUPH
HEH HEH

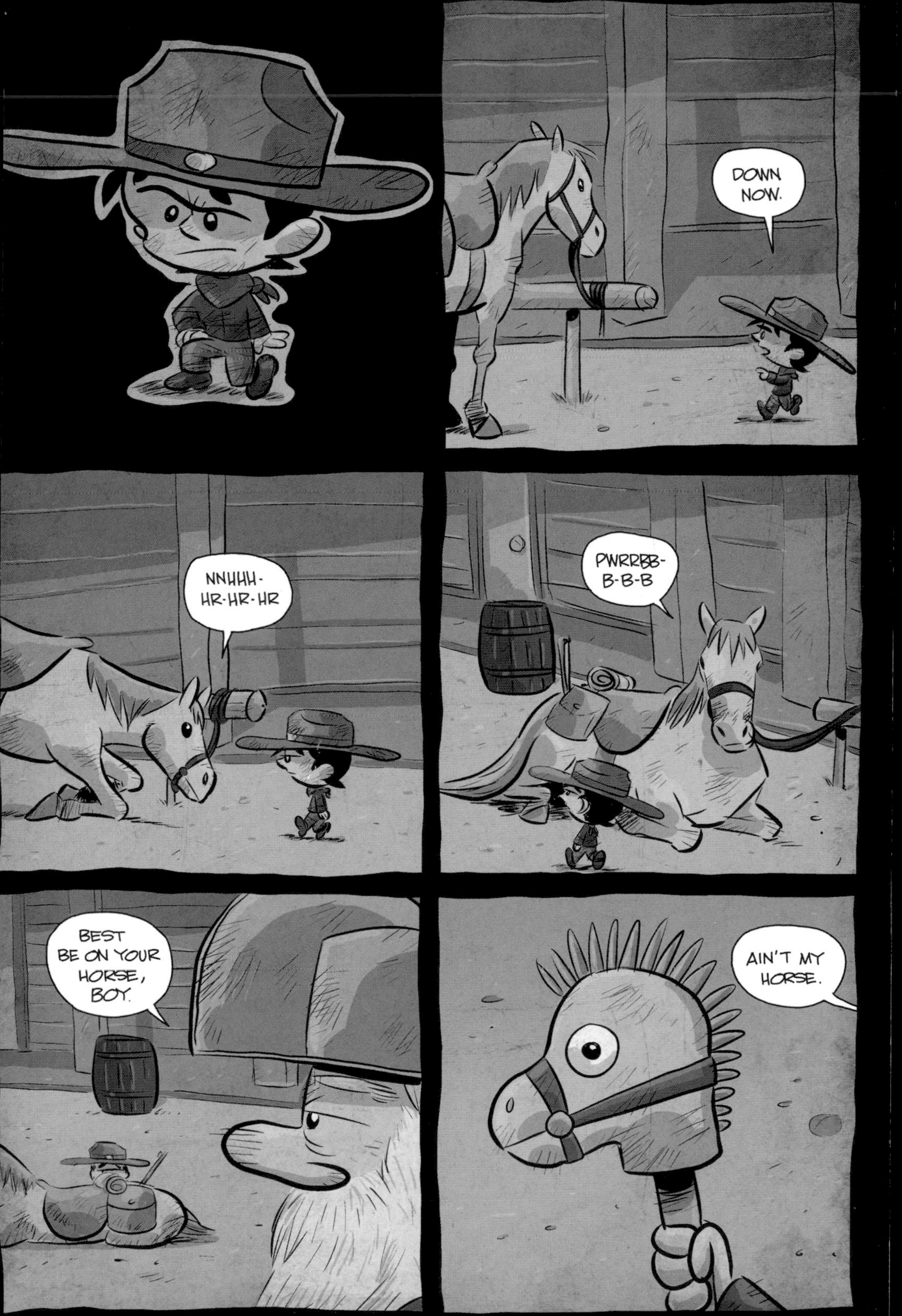
DOWN NOW.
NNHHH-HR-HR-HR
PWRRBB-B-B-B
BEST BE ON YOUR HORSE, BOY.
AIN'T MY HORSE.

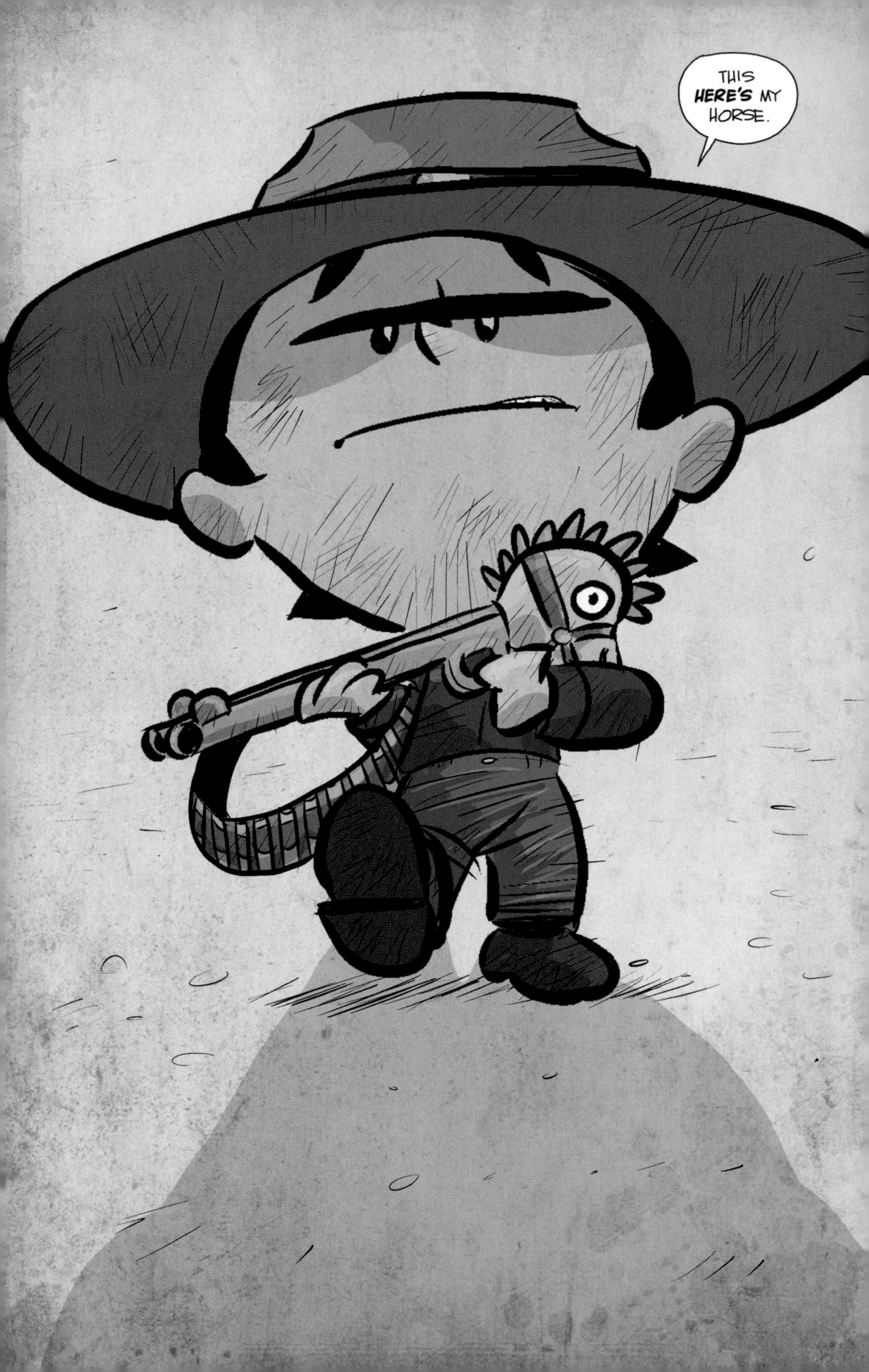
THIS HERE'S MY HORSE.

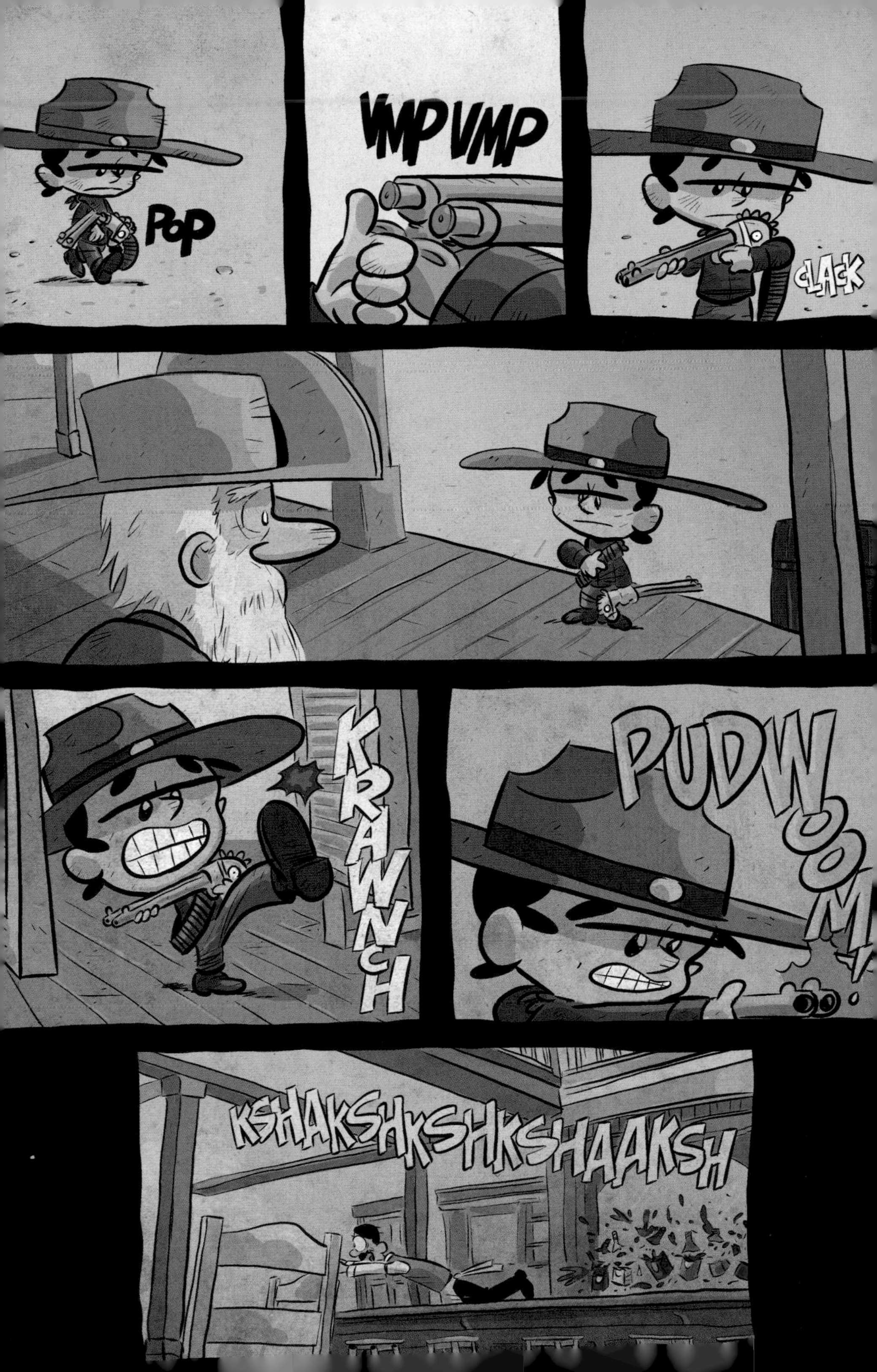
POP
VMP VMP
CLACK
KRAWNCH
PUDWOOOM!
KSHAKSHKSHKSHAAKSH

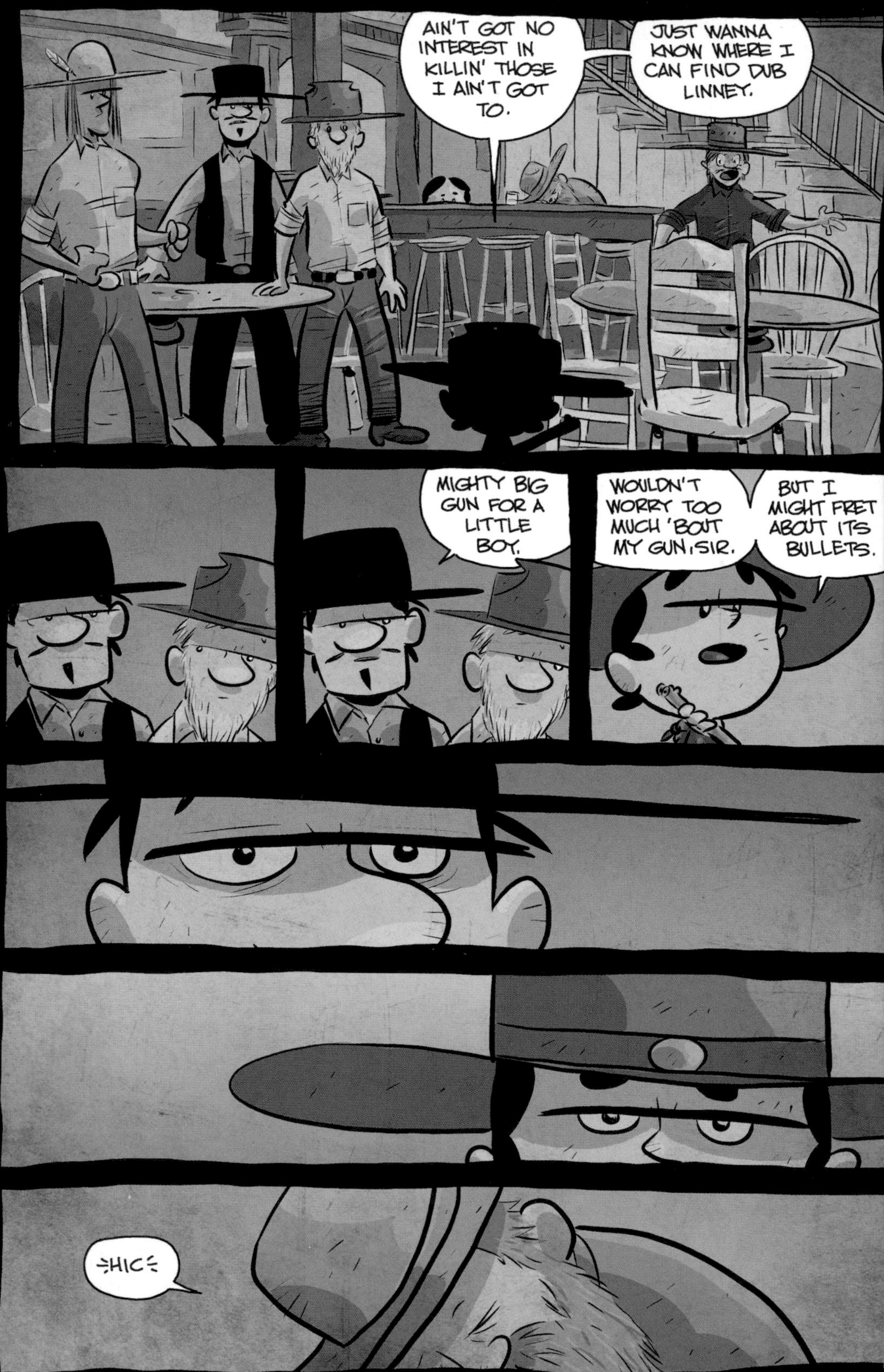
AIN'T GOT NO INTEREST IN KILLIN' THOSE I AIN'T GOT TO.
JUST WANNA KNOW WHERE I CAN FIND DUB LINNEY.
MIGHTY BIG GUN FOR A LITTLE BOY.
WOULDN'T WORRY TOO MUCH 'BOUT MY GUN, SIR.
BUT I MIGHT FRET ABOUT ITS BULLETS.
HIC

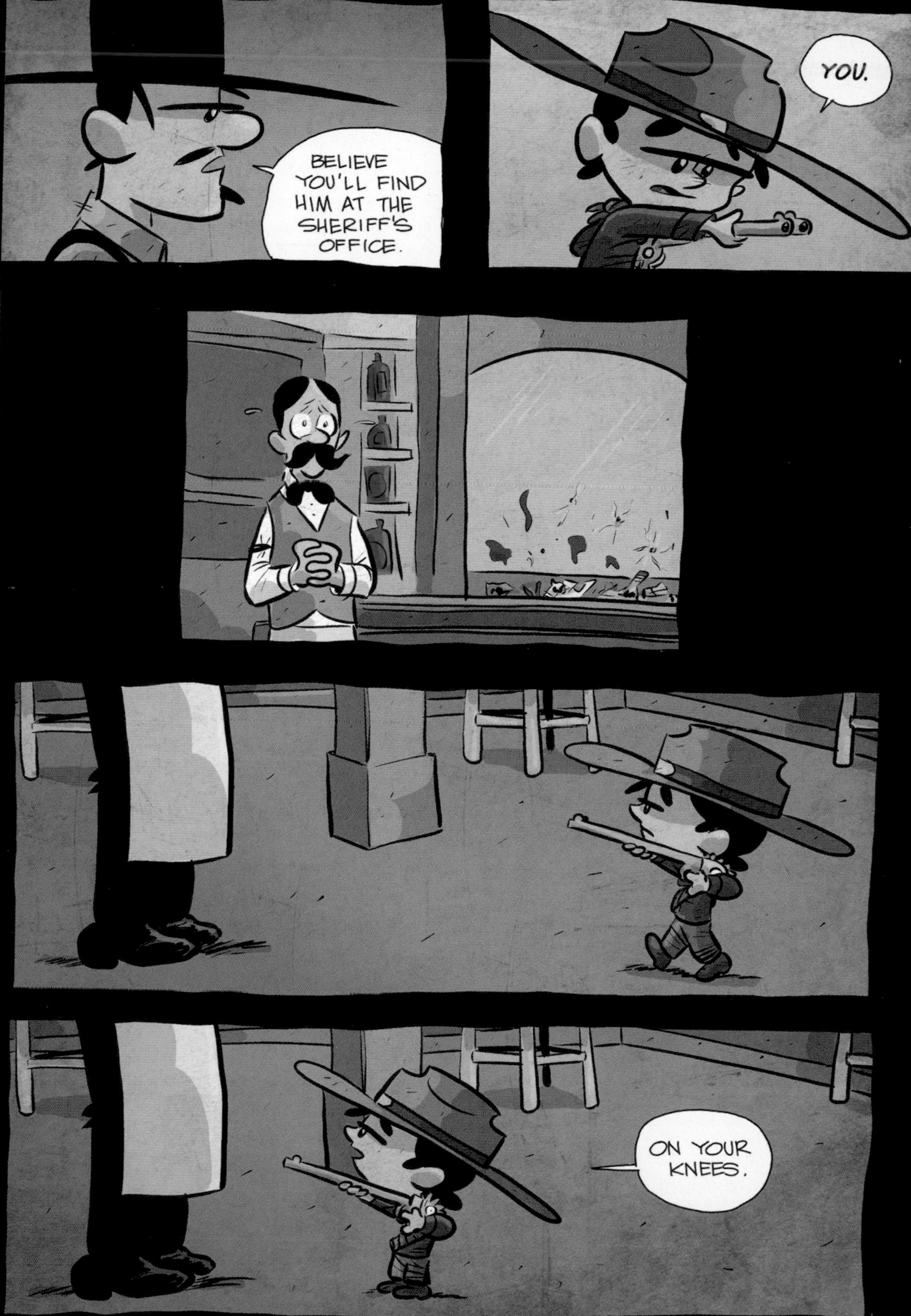
BELIEVE YOU'LL FIND HIM AT THE SHERIFF'S OFFICE.
YOU.
ON YOUR KNEES.

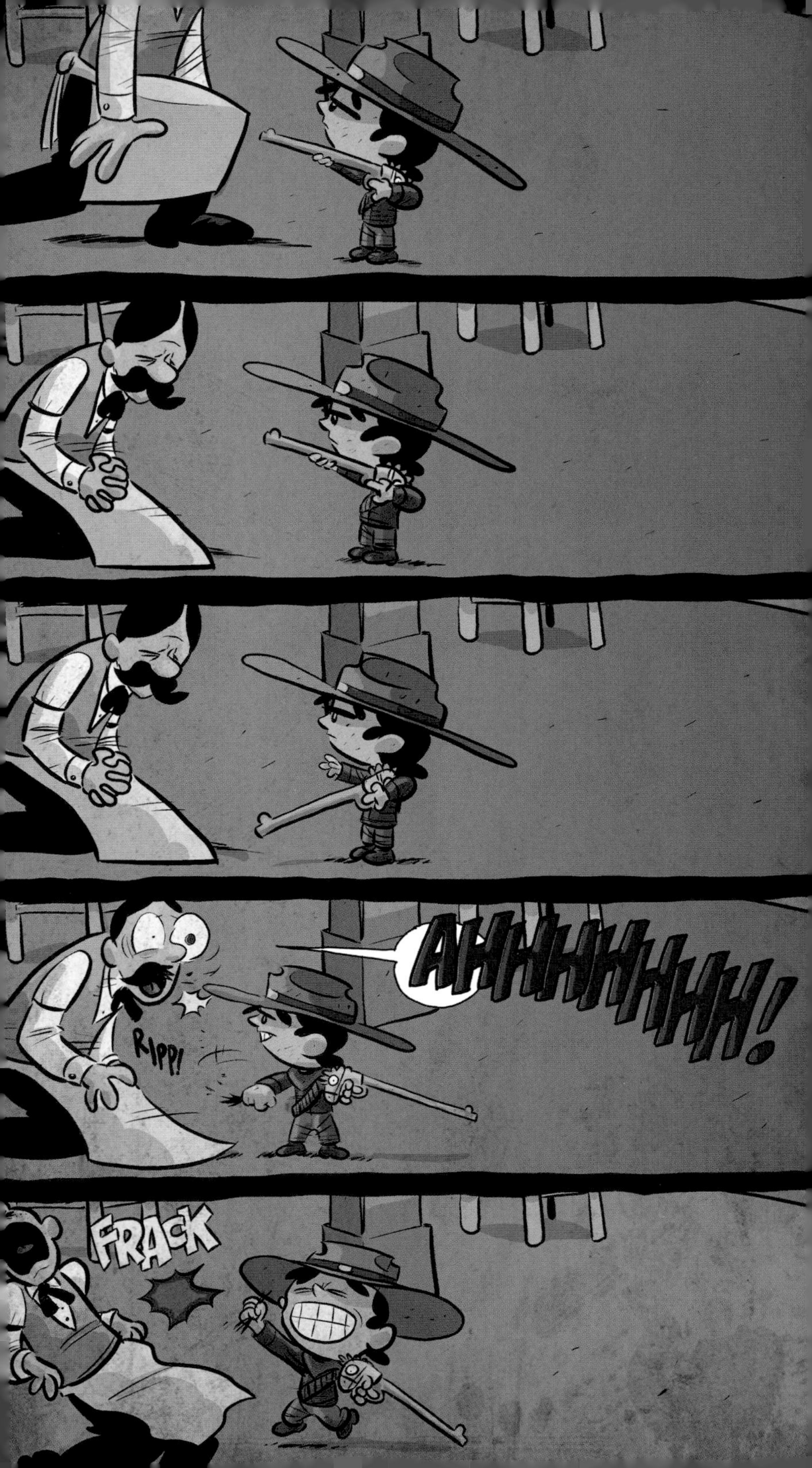
AHHHHHHHH!
RIPP!
FRACK

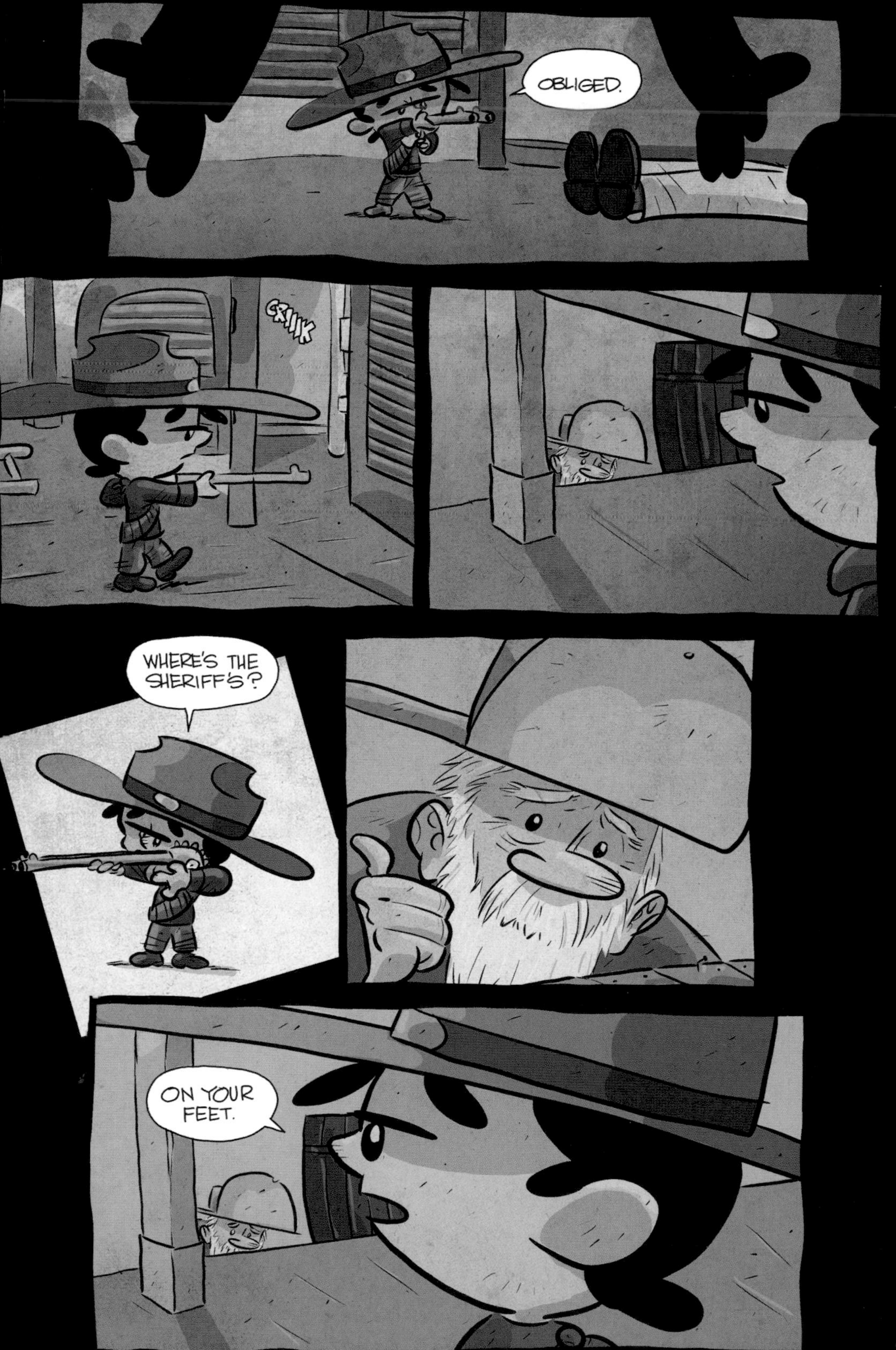
OBLIGED.
CRIIIK
WHERE'S THE SHERIFF'S?
ON YOUR FEET.

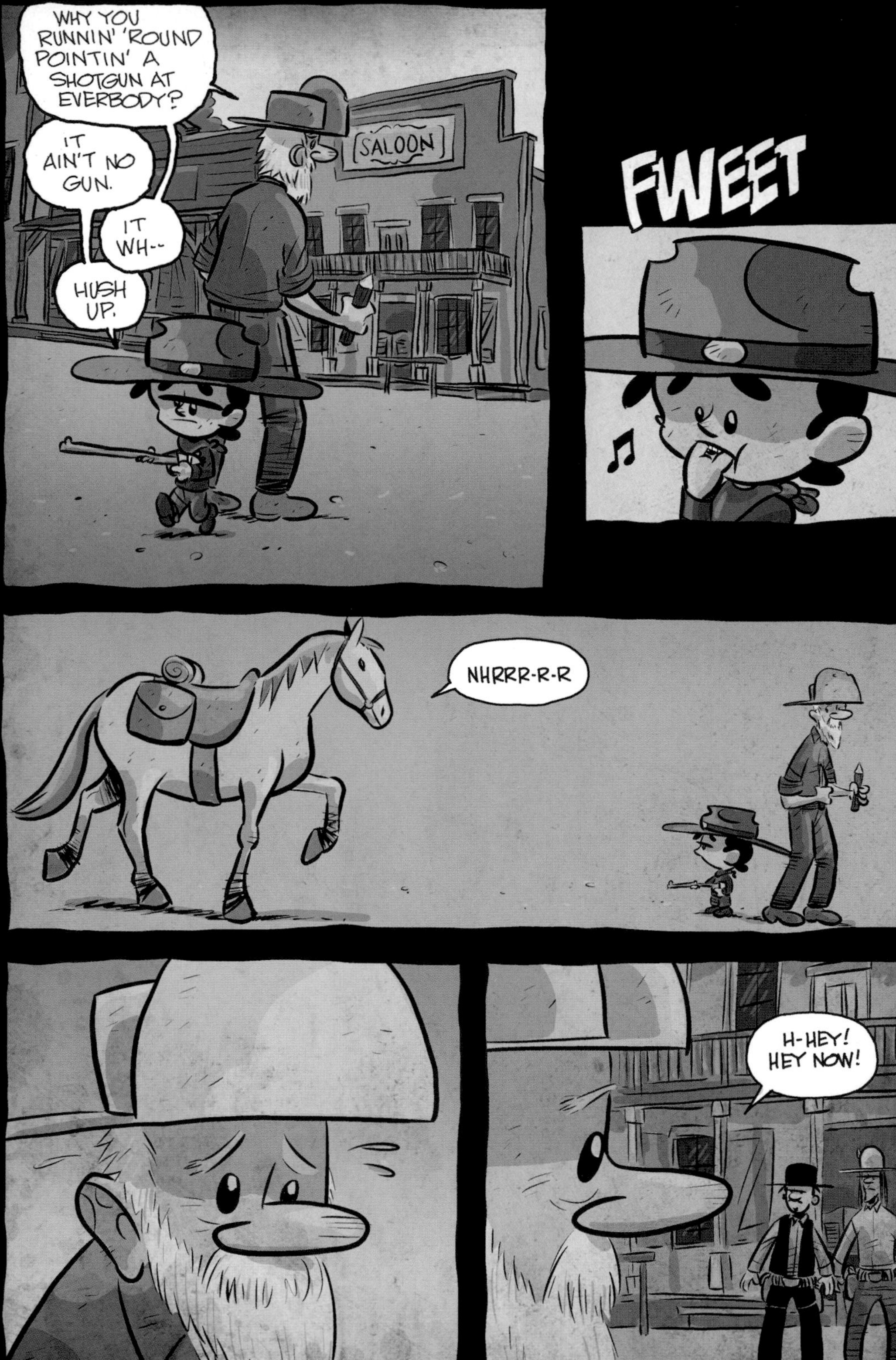
WHY YOU RUNNIN' 'ROUND POINTIN' A SHOTGUN AT EVERBODY?
IT AIN'T NO GUN.
IT WH--
HUSH UP.
SALOON
FWEET
NHRRR-R-R
H-HEY! HEY NOW!

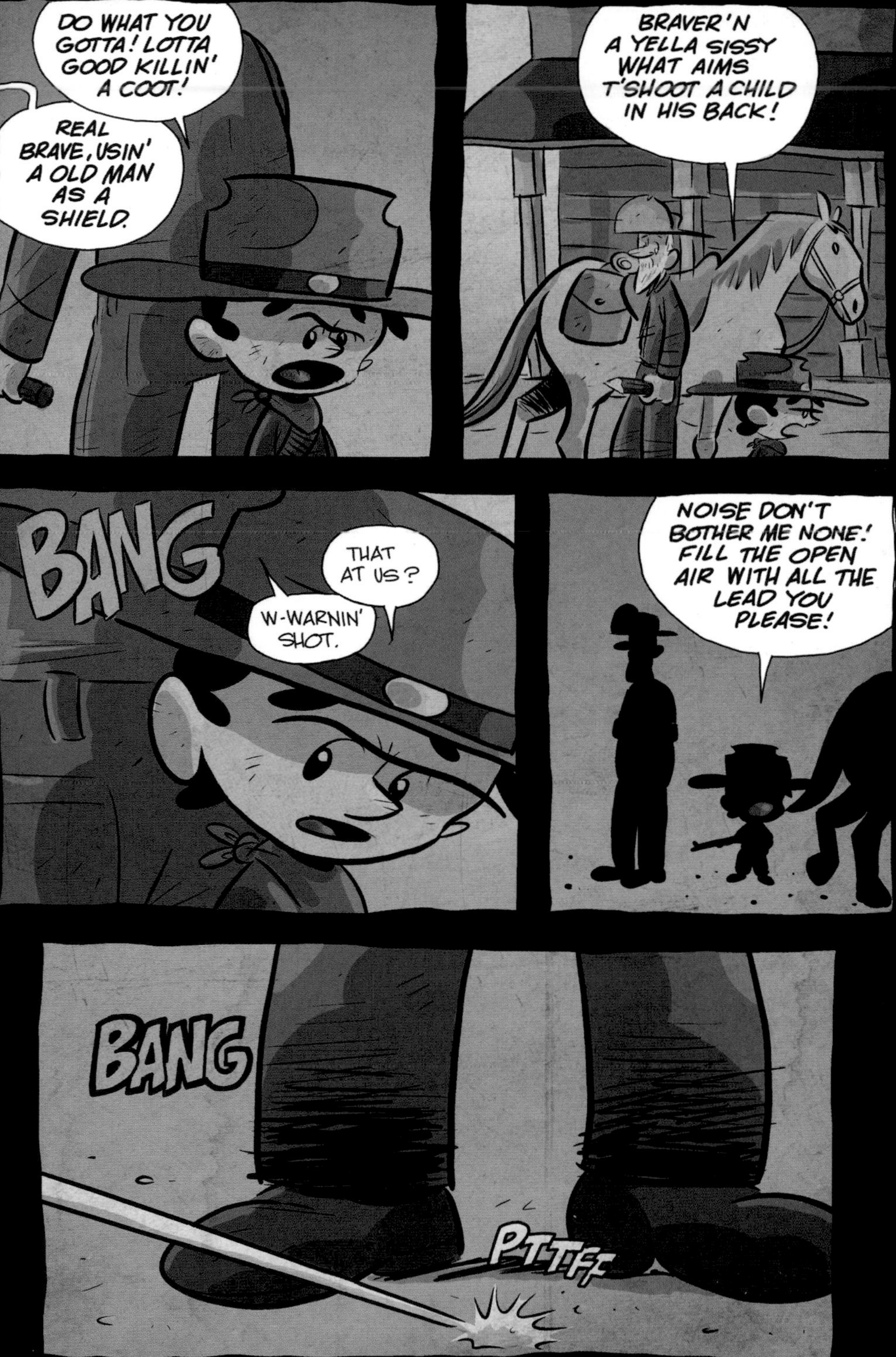
DO WHAT YOU GOTTA! LOTTA GOOD KILLIN' A COOT!
REAL BRAVE, USIN' A OLD MAN AS A SHIELD.
BRAVER'N A YELLA SISSY WHAT AIMS T'SHOOT A CHILD IN HIS BACK!
BANG
THAT AT US?
W-WARNIN' SHOT.
NOISE DON'T BOTHER ME NONE! FILL THE OPEN AIR WITH ALL THE LEAD YOU PLEASE!
BANG
PTTFF

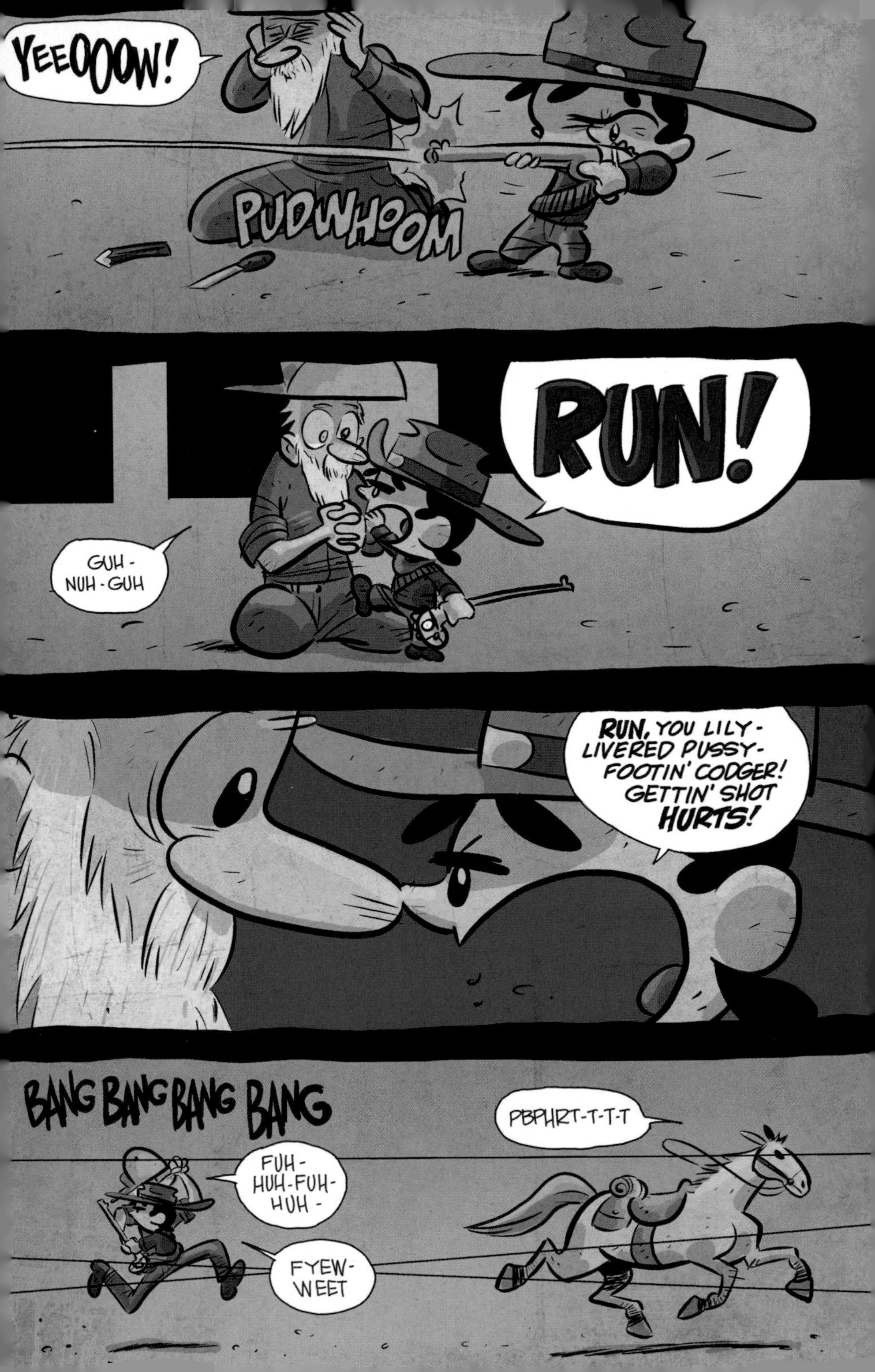
YEEOOOW!
PUDWHOOM
RUN!
GUH-
NUH-GUH
RUN, YOU LILY-LIVERED PUSSY-FOOTIN' CODGER! GETTIN' SHOT HURTS!
BANG BANG BANG BANG
PBPHRT-T-T-T
FUH-
HUH-FUH-
HUH-
FYEW-
WEET

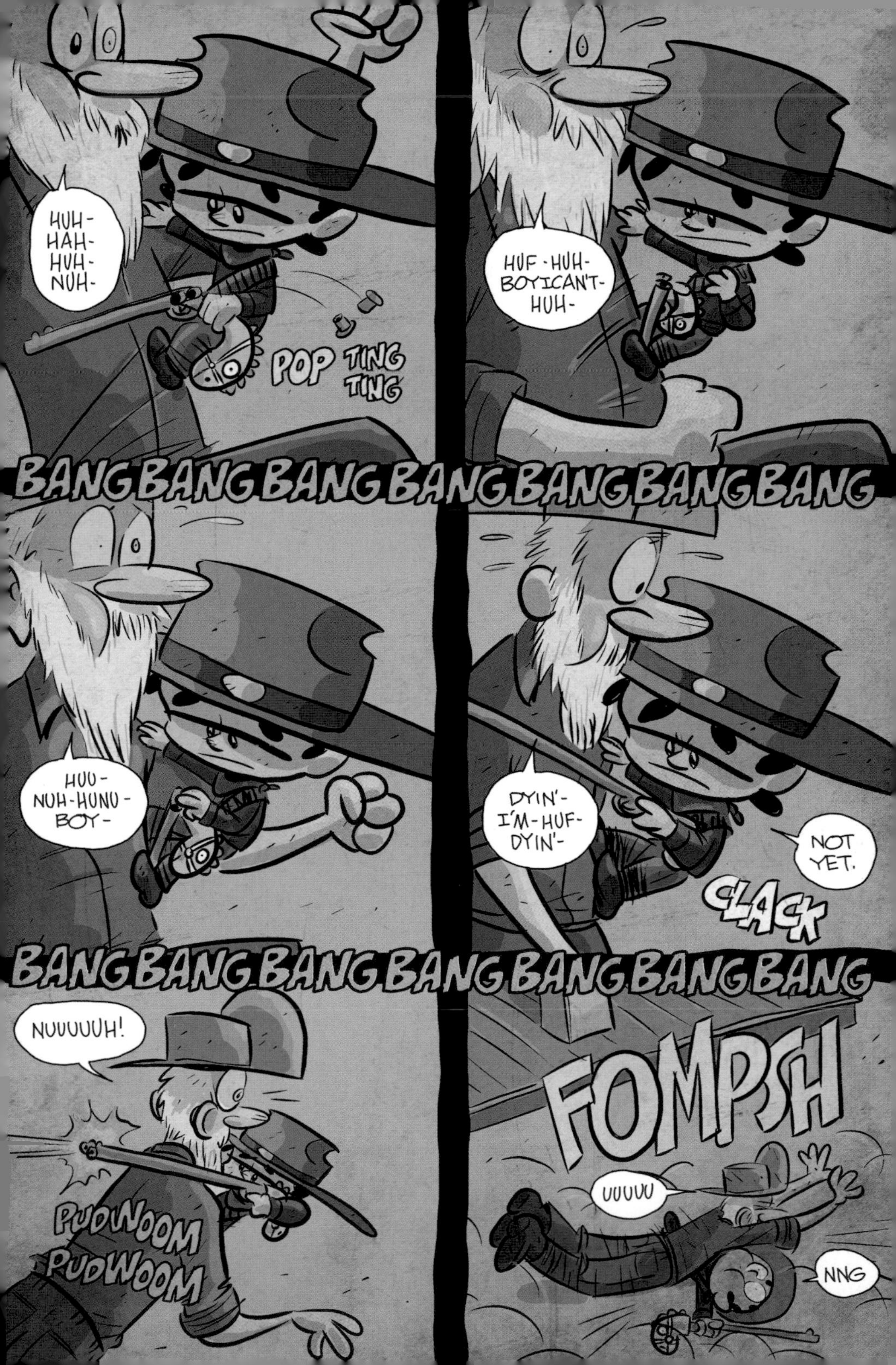
HUH-
HAH-
HUH-
NUH-
POP TING TING
HUF-HUH-
BOY I CAN'T-
HUH-
BANG BANG BANG BANG BANG BANG BANG
HUU-
NUH-HUNU-
BOY-
DYIN'-
I'M-HUF-
DYIN'-
NOT YET.
CLACK
BANG BANG BANG BANG BANG BANG BANG
NUUUUUH!
PUDWOOM
PUDWOOM
FOMPSH
UUUUU
NNG

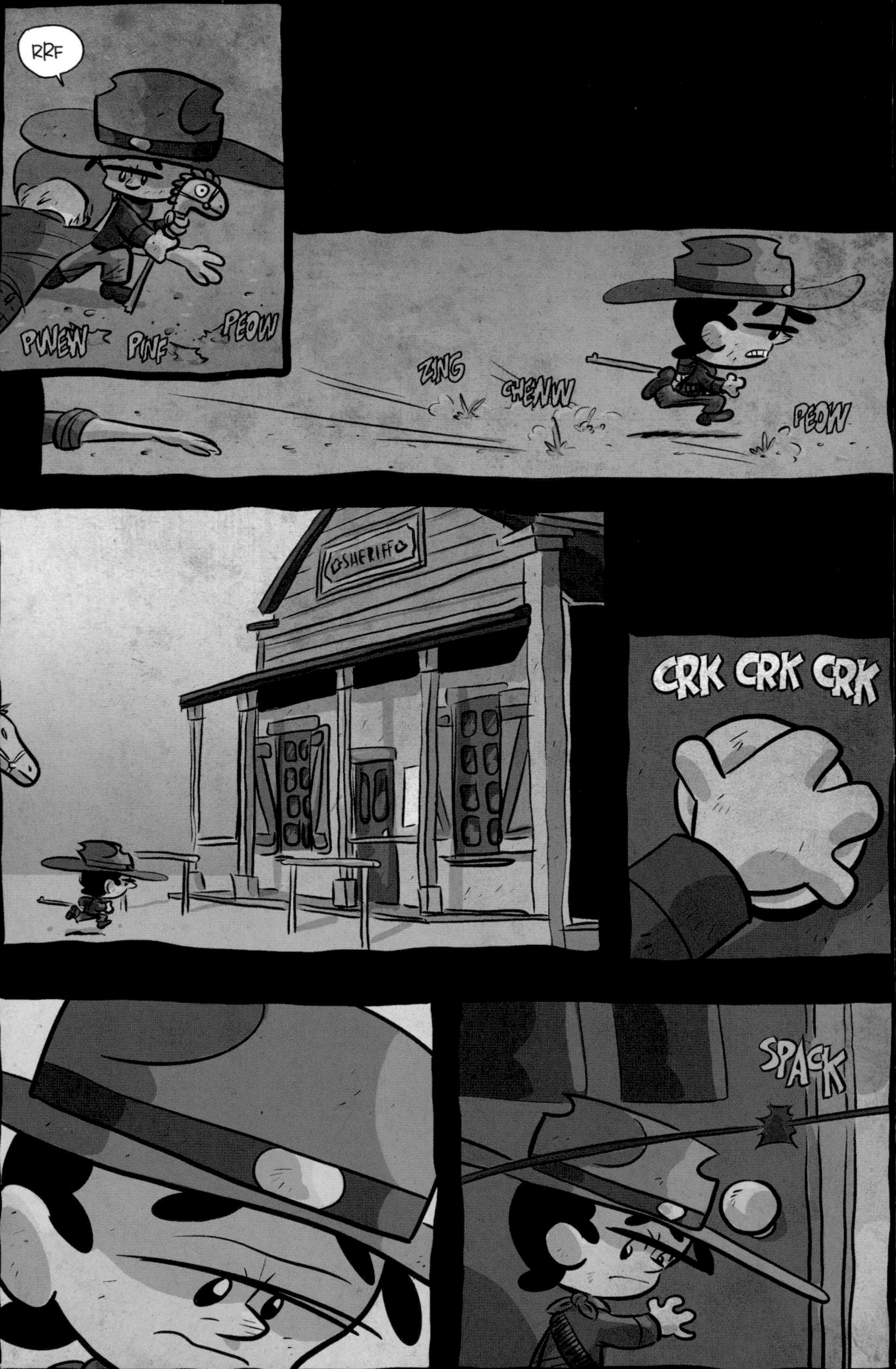
RRF
PWEW
PINF
PEOW
ZING
CHEWW
PEOW
SHERIFF
CRK CRK CRK
SPACK

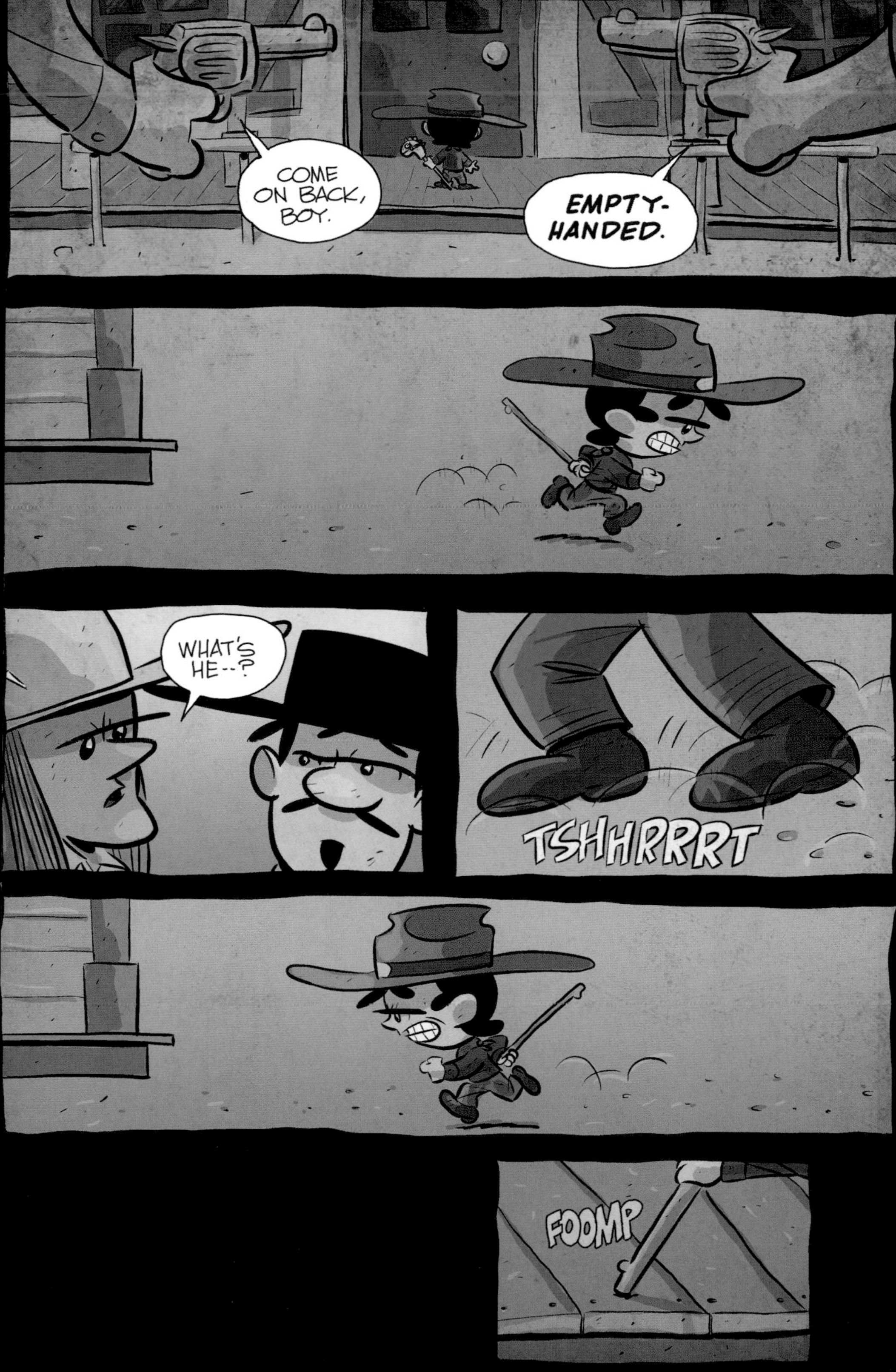
COME ON BACK, BOY.
EMPTY-HANDED.
WHAT'S HE--?
TSHHRRRT
FOOMP

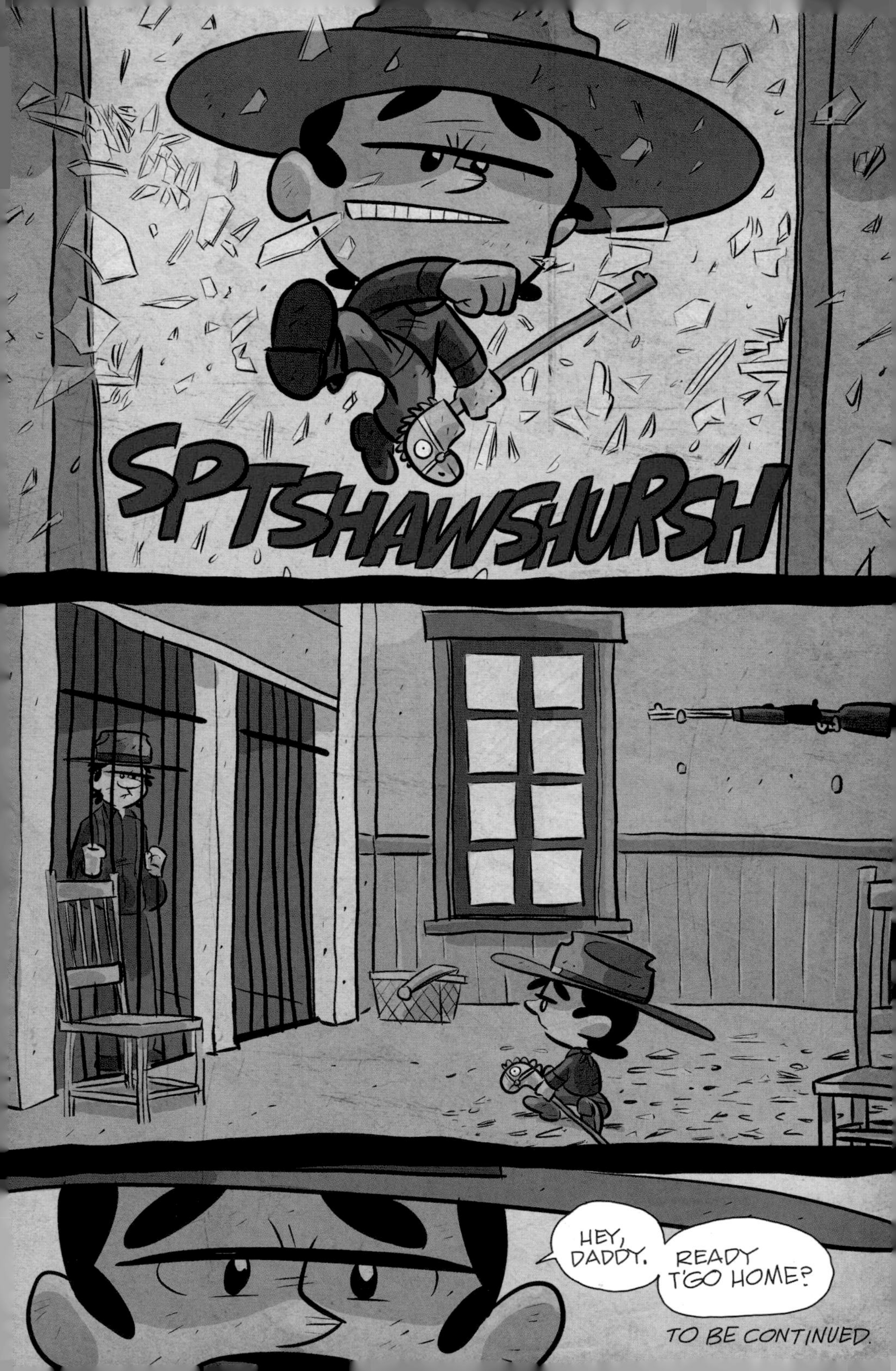
SPTSHAWSHURSH
HEY, DADDY.
READY T'GO HOME?
TO BE CONTINUED.

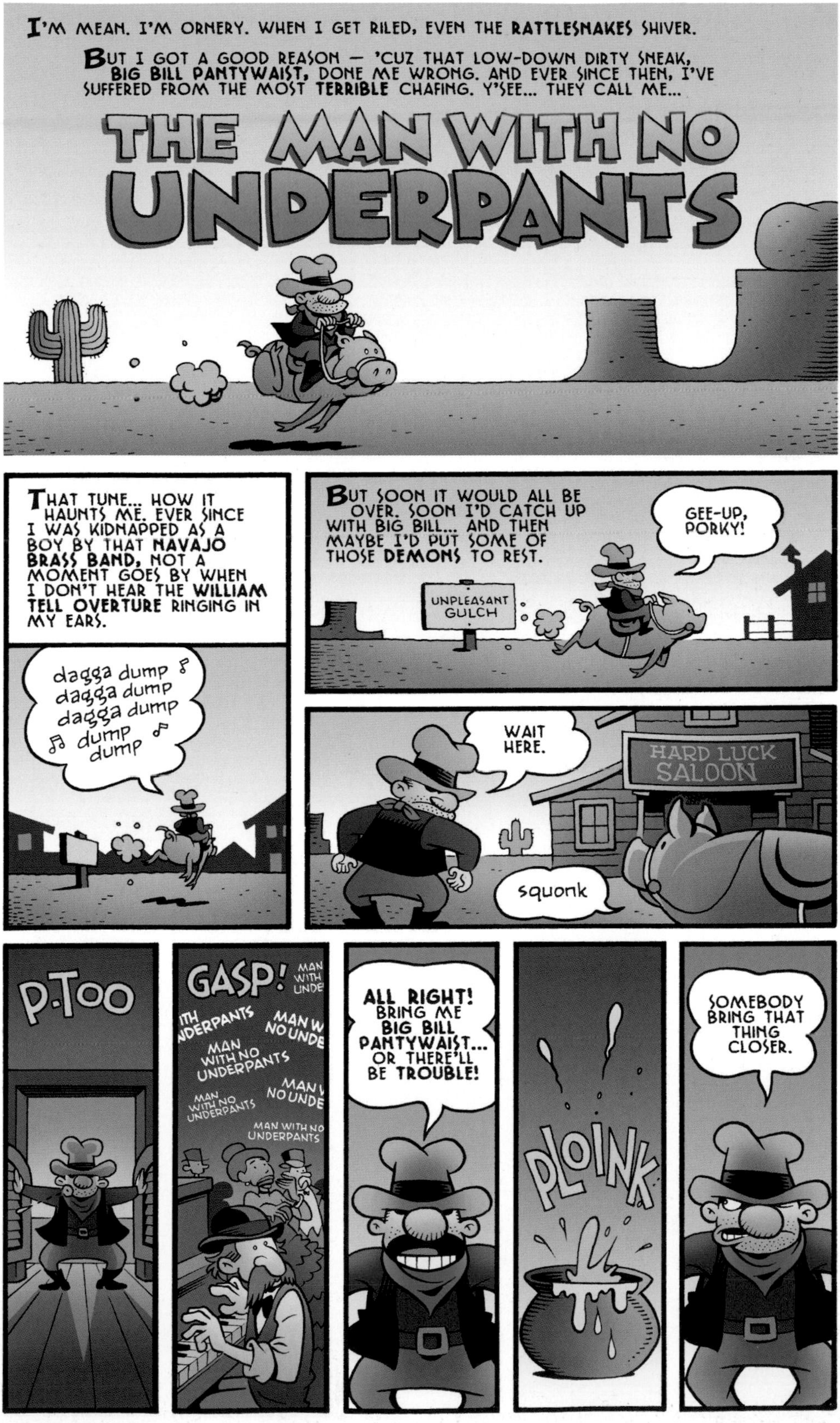
I'M MEAN. I'M ORNERY. WHEN I GET RILED, EVEN THE RATTLESNAKES SHIVER.
BUT I GOT A GOOD REASON — 'CUZ THAT LOW-DOWN DIRTY SNEAK, BIG BILL PANTYWAIST, DONE ME WRONG. AND EVER SINCE THEN, I'VE SUFFERED FROM THE MOST TERRIBLE CHAFING. Y'SEE... THEY CALL ME...
THE MAN WITH NO UNDERPANTS
THAT TUNE... HOW IT HAUNTS ME. EVER SINCE I WAS KIDNAPPED AS A BOY BY THAT NAVAJO BRASS BAND, NOT A MOMENT GOES BY WHEN I DON'T HEAR THE WILLIAM TELL OVERTURE RINGING IN MY EARS.
dagga dump dagga dump dagga dump dump dump
BUT SOON IT WOULD ALL BE OVER. SOON I'D CATCH UP WITH BIG BILL... AND THEN MAYBE I'D PUT SOME OF THOSE DEMONS TO REST.
GEE-UP, PORKY!
UNPLEASANT GULCH
WAIT HERE.
HARD LUCK SALOON
squonk
P-TOO
GASP!
MAN WITH NO UNDERPANTS
ALL RIGHT! BRING ME BIG BILL PANTYWAIST... OR THERE'LL BE TROUBLE!
PLOINK
SOMEBODY BRING THAT THING CLOSER.

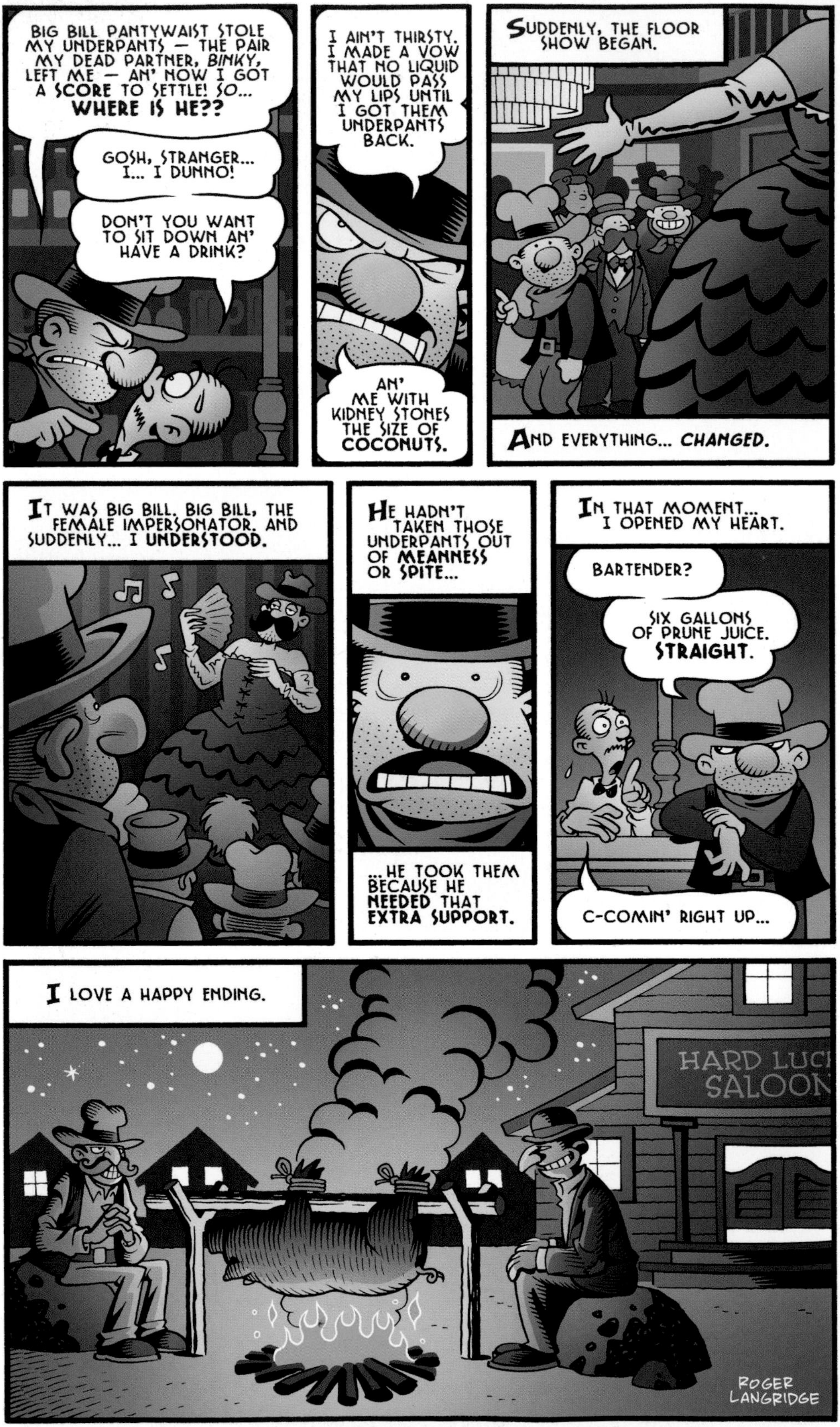
BIG BILL PANTYWAIST STOLE MY UNDERPANTS — THE PAIR MY DEAD PARTNER, *BINKY*, LEFT ME — AN' NOW I GOT A **SCORE** TO SETTLE! *SO*... **WHERE IS HE??**
GOSH, STRANGER... I... I DUNNO!
DON'T YOU WANT TO SIT DOWN AN' HAVE A DRINK?
I AIN'T THIRSTY. I MADE A VOW THAT NO LIQUID WOULD PASS MY LIPS UNTIL I GOT THEM UNDERPANTS BACK.
AN' ME WITH KIDNEY STONES THE SIZE OF **COCONUTS**.
SUDDENLY, THE FLOOR SHOW BEGAN.
AND EVERYTHING... ***CHANGED***.
IT WAS BIG BILL. BIG BILL, THE FEMALE IMPERSONATOR. AND SUDDENLY... I **UNDERSTOOD**.
HE HADN'T TAKEN THOSE UNDERPANTS OUT OF **MEANNESS** OR **SPITE**...
...HE TOOK THEM BECAUSE HE **NEEDED** THAT **EXTRA SUPPORT**.
IN THAT MOMENT... I OPENED MY HEART.
BARTENDER?
SIX GALLONS OF PRUNE JUICE. **STRAIGHT**.
C-COMIN' RIGHT UP...
I LOVE A HAPPY ENDING.
HARD LUC
SALOON
ROGER LANGRIDGE

I GOT BORN.

I STIRRED TROUBLE.

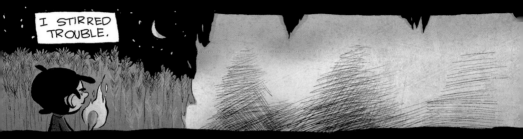

I GOT BEAT.

THOSE ARE THE BASICS OF MY LIFE, FAR BACK AS I CAN REMEMBER.

MAMA LIKED T'SAY I GOT TOO MUCH 'A MY DADDY IN ME.

DADGUMMIT.

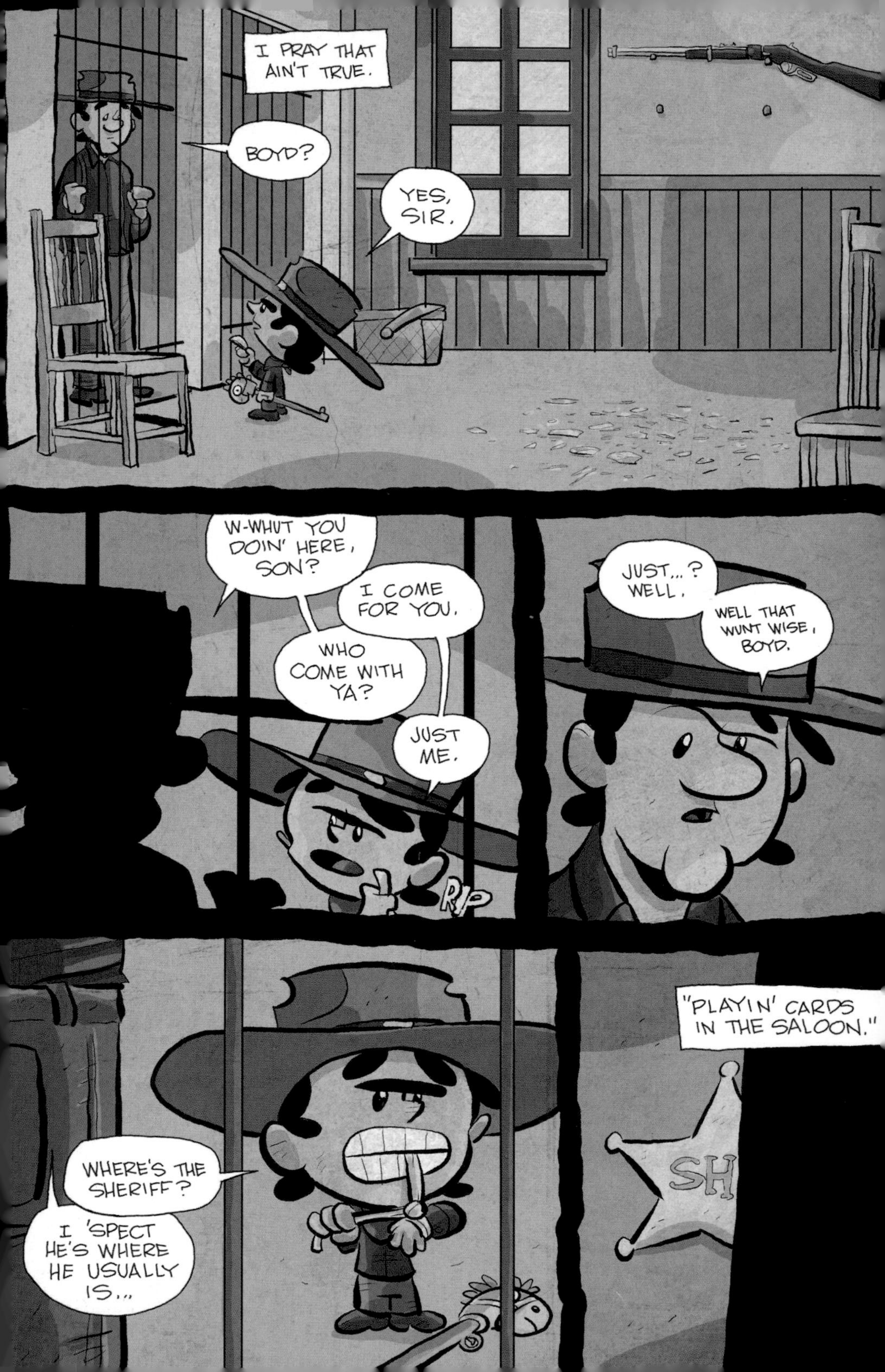

I PRAY THAT AIN'T TRUE.
BOYD?
YES, SIR.
W-WHUT YOU DOIN' HERE, SON?
I COME FOR YOU.
WHO COME WITH YA?
JUST ME.
RIP
JUST... ? WELL.
WELL THAT WUNT WISE, BOYD.
WHERE'S THE SHERIFF?
I 'SPECT HE'S WHERE HE USUALLY IS...
"PLAYIN' CARDS IN THE SALOON."
SH

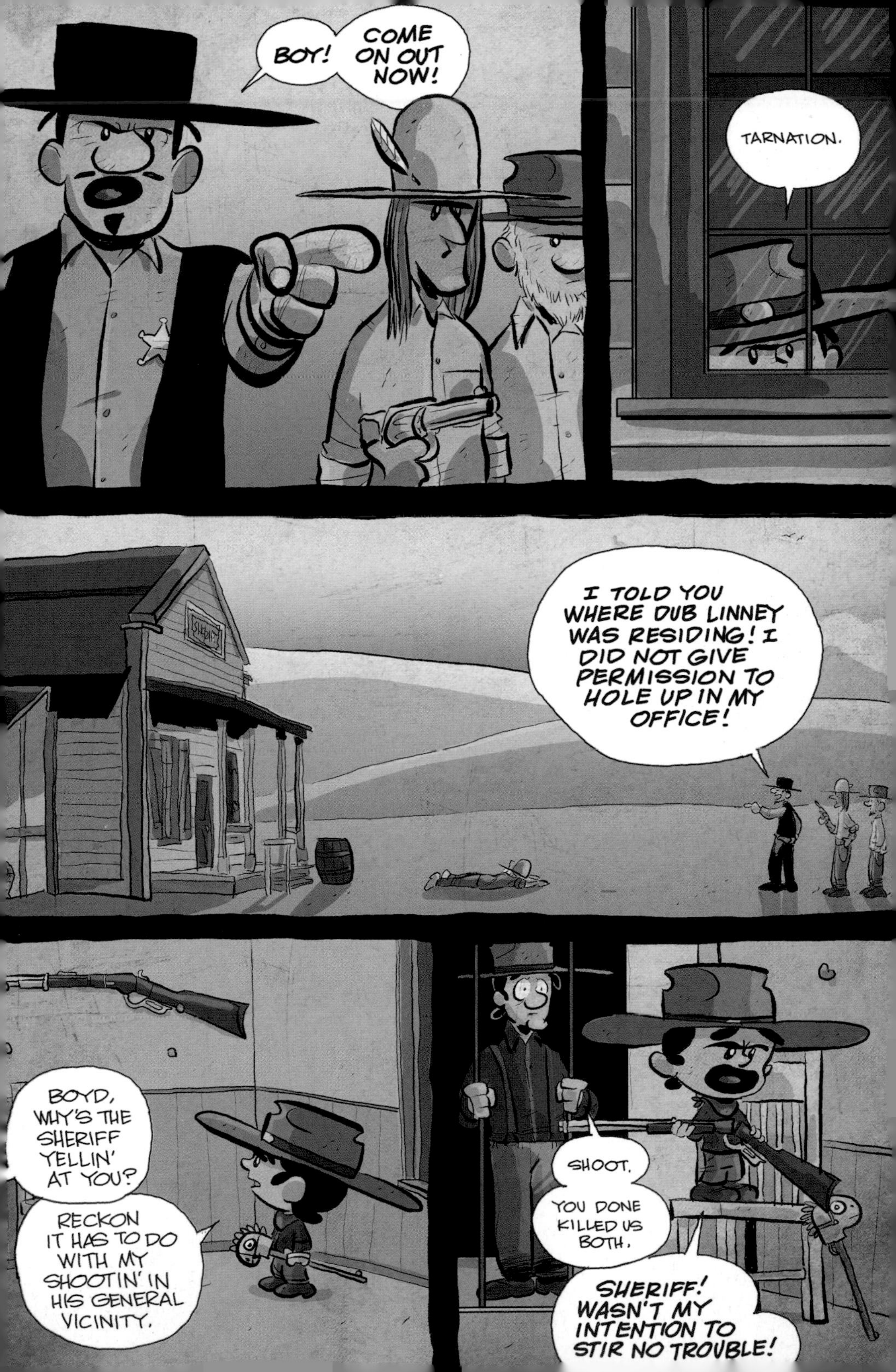
BOY!
COME ON OUT NOW!
TARNATION.
SHERIFF
I TOLD YOU WHERE DUB LINNEY WAS RESIDING! I DID NOT GIVE PERMISSION TO HOLE UP IN MY OFFICE!
BOYD, WHY'S THE SHERIFF YELLIN' AT YOU?
RECKON IT HAS TO DO WITH MY SHOOTIN' IN HIS GENERAL VICINITY.
SHOOT.
YOU DONE KILLED US BOTH.
SHERIFF! WASN'T MY INTENTION TO STIR NO TROUBLE!

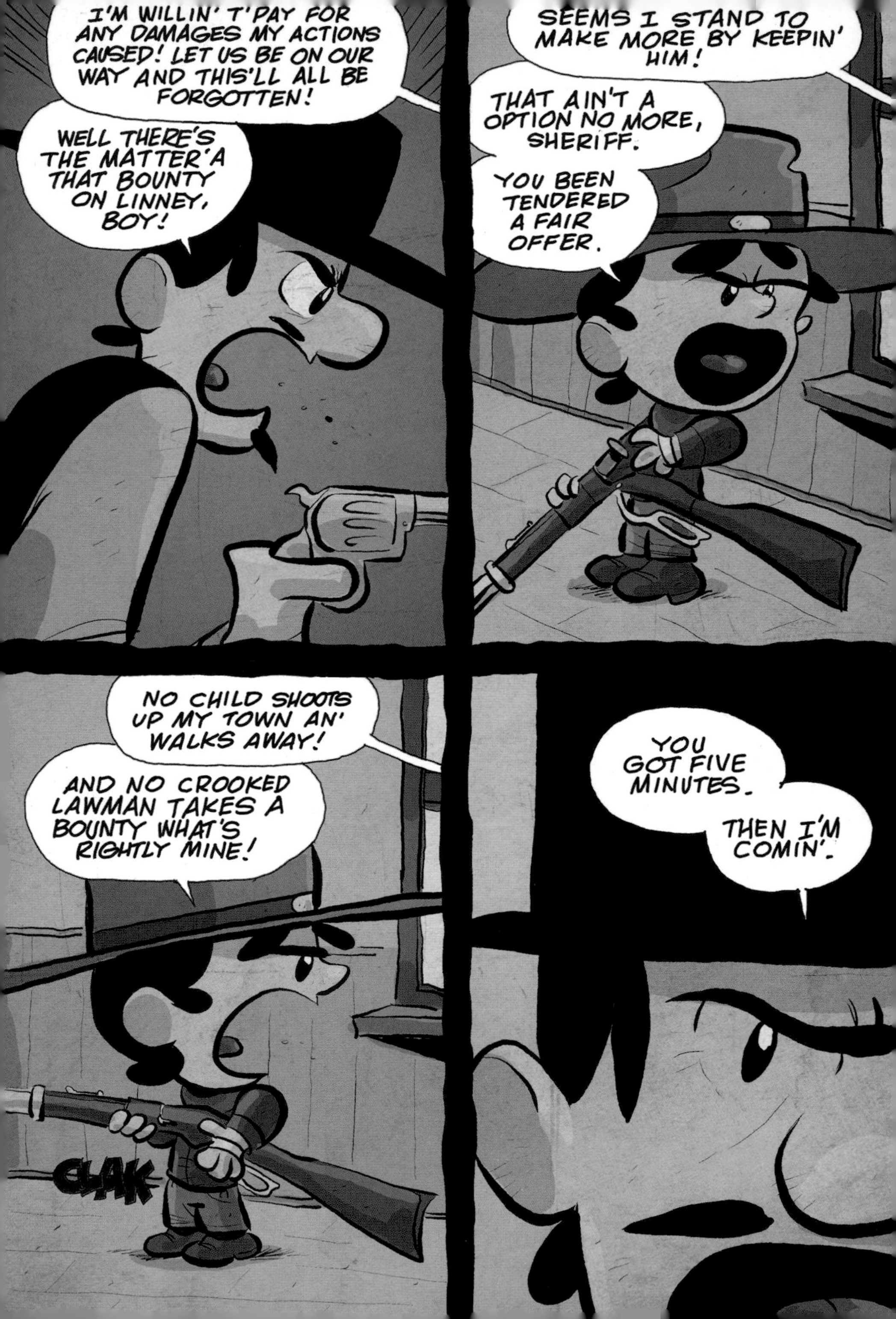
I'M WILLIN' T'PAY FOR ANY DAMAGES MY ACTIONS CAUSED! LET US BE ON OUR WAY AND THIS'LL ALL BE FORGOTTEN!
WELL THERE'S THE MATTER'A THAT BOUNTY ON LINNEY, BOY!
SEEMS I STAND TO MAKE MORE BY KEEPIN' HIM!
THAT AIN'T A OPTION NO MORE, SHERIFF.
YOU BEEN TENDERED A FAIR OFFER.
NO CHILD SHOOTS UP MY TOWN AN' WALKS AWAY!
AND NO CROOKED LAWMAN TAKES A BOUNTY WHAT'S RIGHTLY MINE!
CLAK
YOU GOT FIVE MINUTES.
THEN I'M COMIN'.

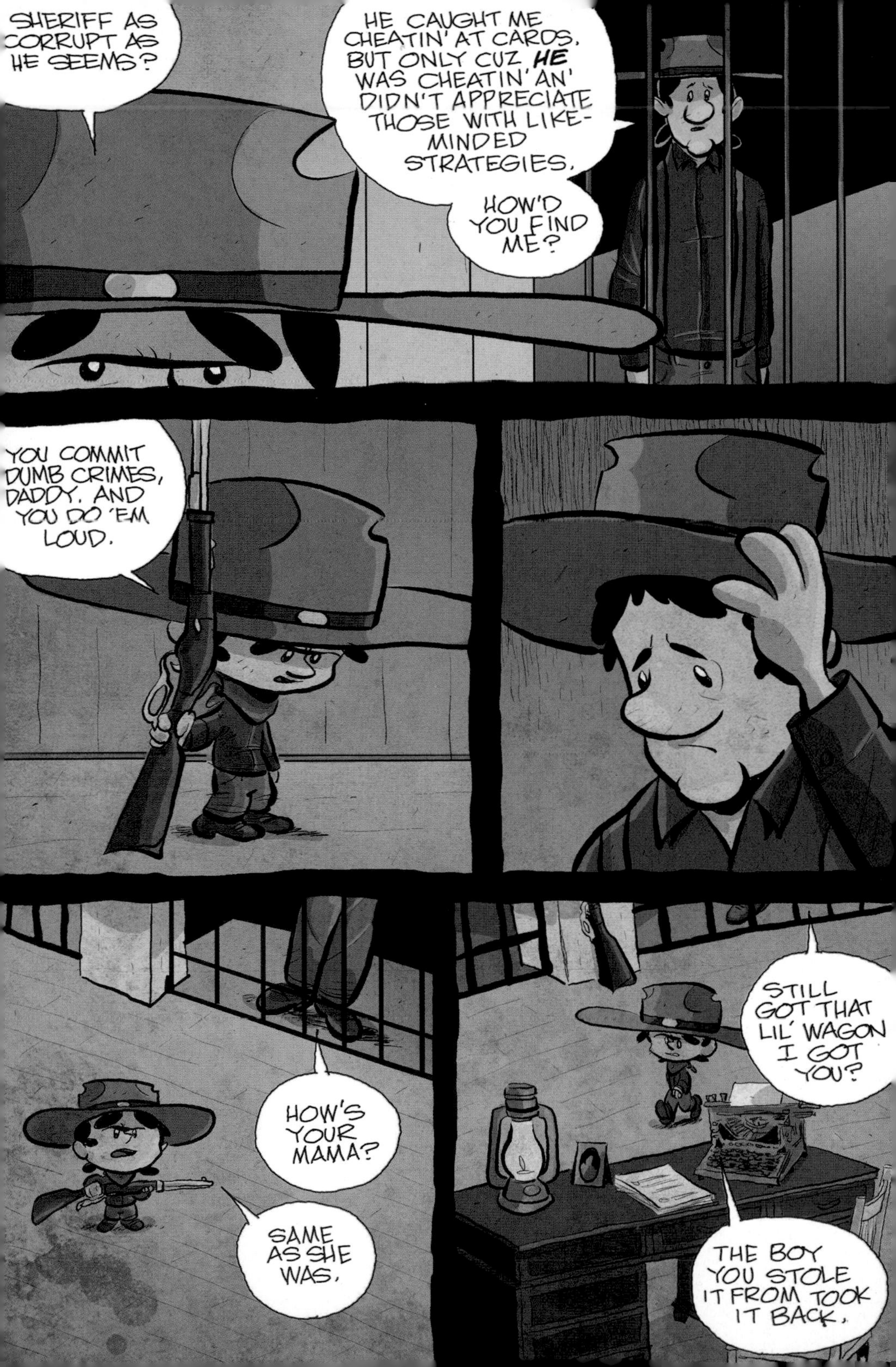
SHERIFF AS CORRUPT AS HE SEEMS?
HE CAUGHT ME CHEATIN' AT CARDS, BUT ONLY CUZ **HE** WAS CHEATIN' AN' DIDN'T APPRECIATE THOSE WITH LIKE-MINDED STRATEGIES.
HOW'D YOU FIND ME?
YOU COMMIT DUMB CRIMES, DADDY, AND YOU DO 'EM LOUD.
HOW'S YOUR MAMA?
SAME AS SHE WAS.
STILL GOT THAT LIL' WAGON I GOT YOU?
THE BOY YOU STOLE IT FROM TOOK IT BACK.

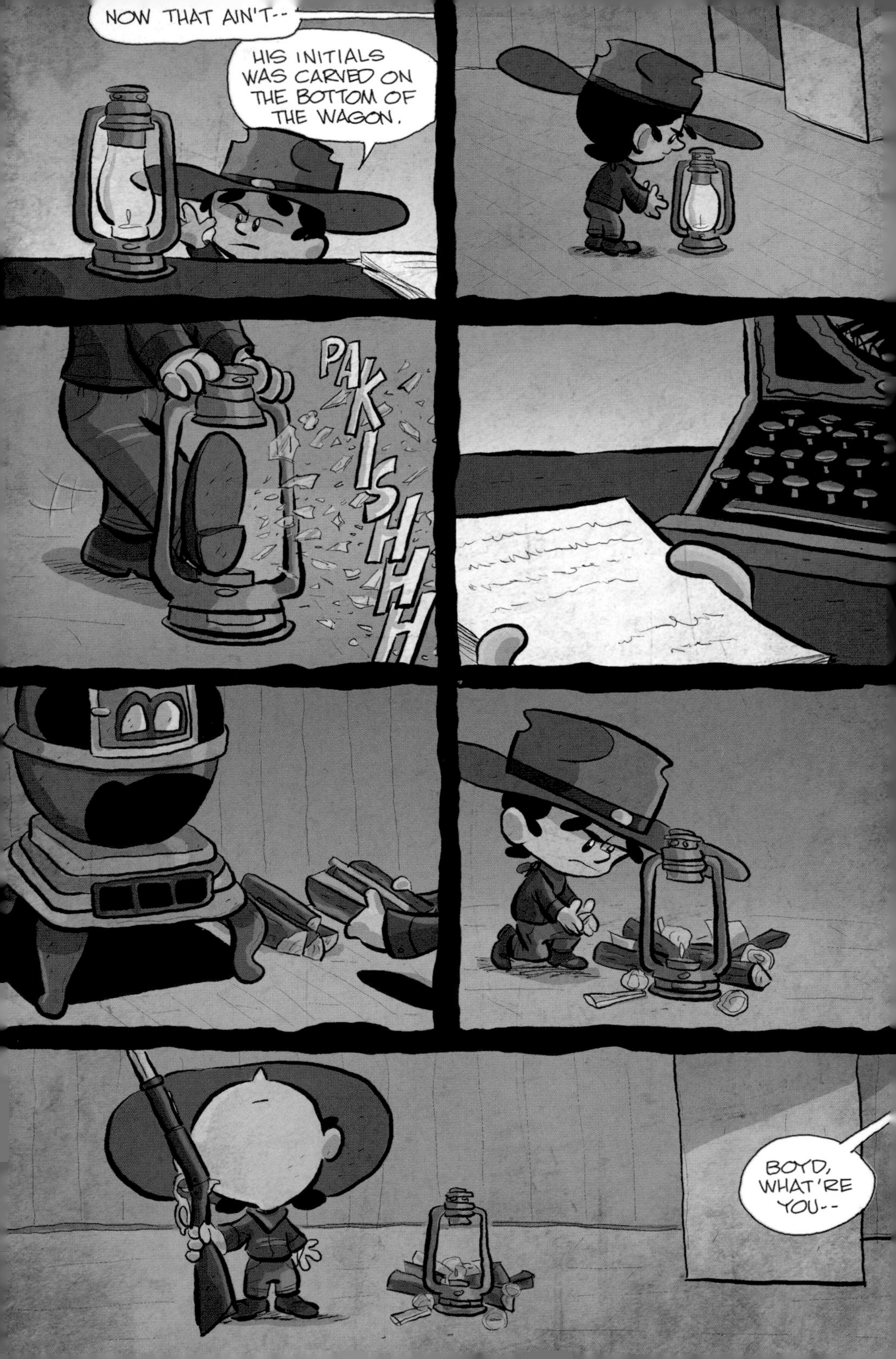
NOW THAT AIN'T--
HIS INITIALS WAS CARVED ON THE BOTTOM OF THE WAGON.
PAKISHHHH
BOYD, WHAT'RE YOU--

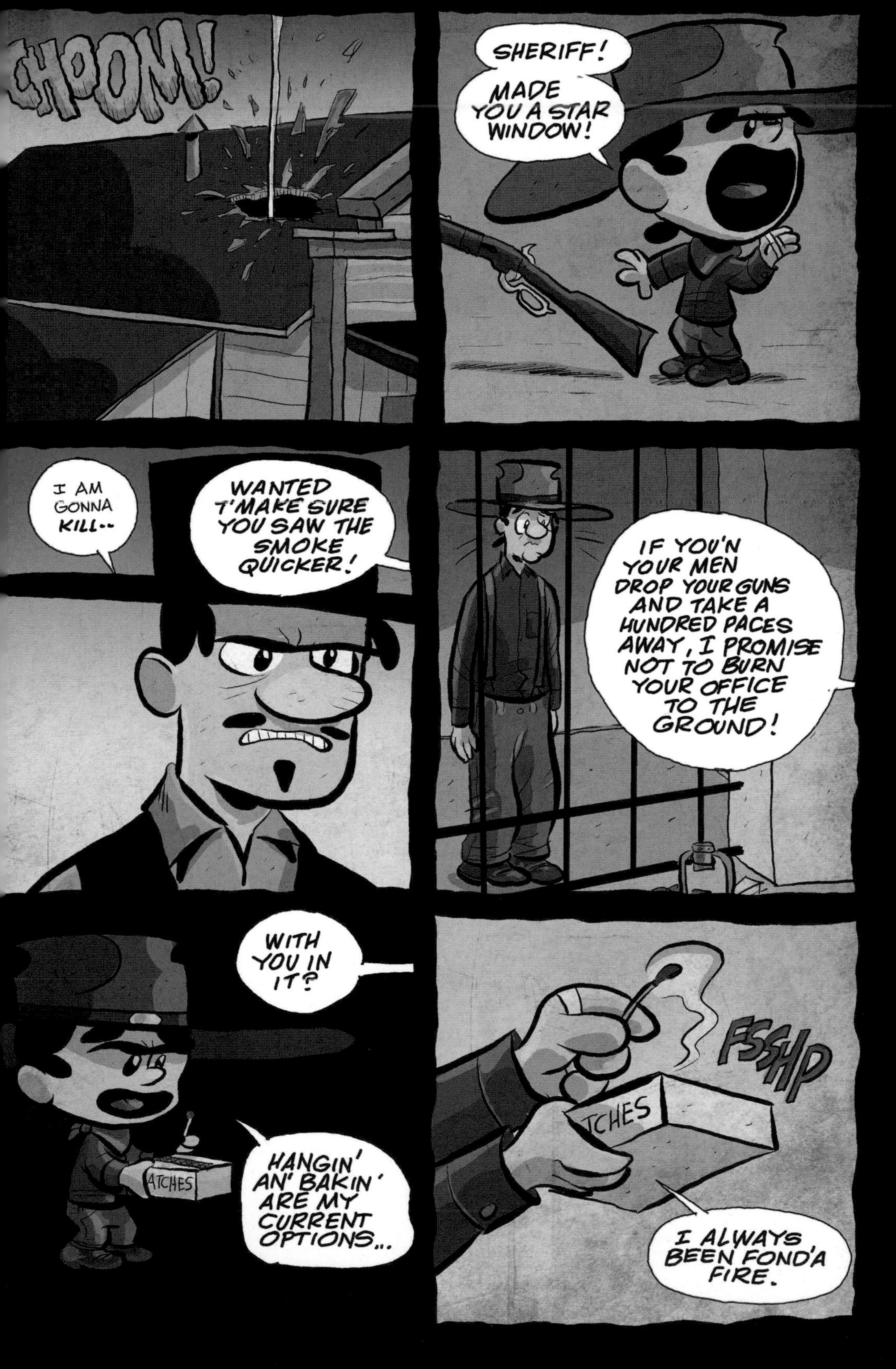
CHOOM!
SHERIFF!
MADE YOU A STAR WINDOW!
I AM GONNA KILL..
WANTED T'MAKE SURE YOU SAW THE SMOKE QUICKER!
IF YOU'N YOUR MEN DROP YOUR GUNS AND TAKE A HUNDRED PACES AWAY, I PROMISE NOT TO BURN YOUR OFFICE TO THE GROUND!
WITH YOU IN IT?
ATCHES
HANGIN' AN' BAKIN' ARE MY CURRENT OPTIONS...
FSSHP
TCHES
I ALWAYS BEEN FOND'A FIRE.

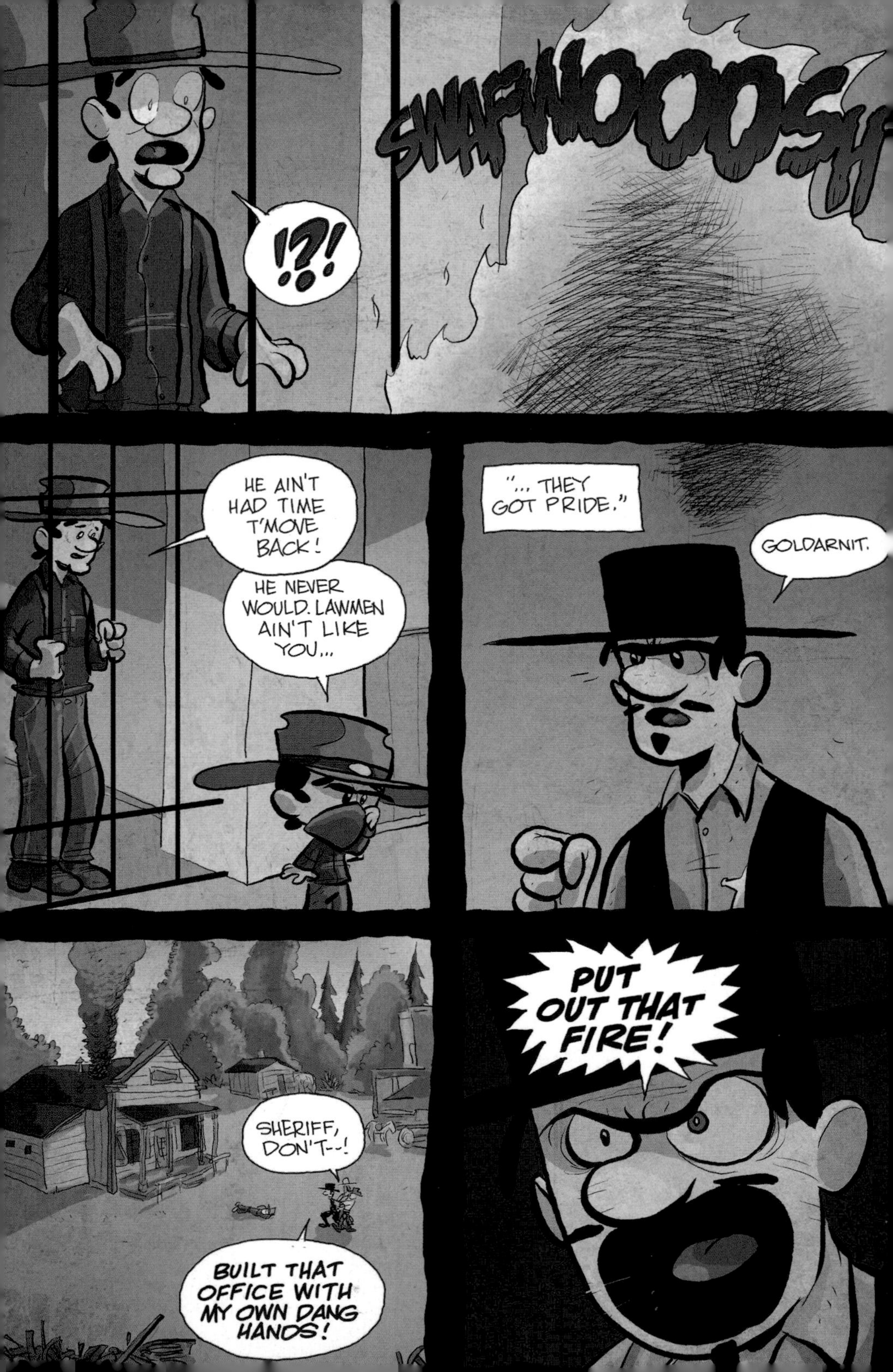
!?!
SNAFWOOOSH
HE AIN'T HAD TIME T'MOVE BACK!
HE NEVER WOULD. LAWMEN AIN'T LIKE YOU...
"... THEY GOT PRIDE."
GOLDARNIT.
SHERIFF, DON'T--!
BUILT THAT OFFICE WITH MY OWN DANG HANDS!
PUT OUT THAT FIRE!

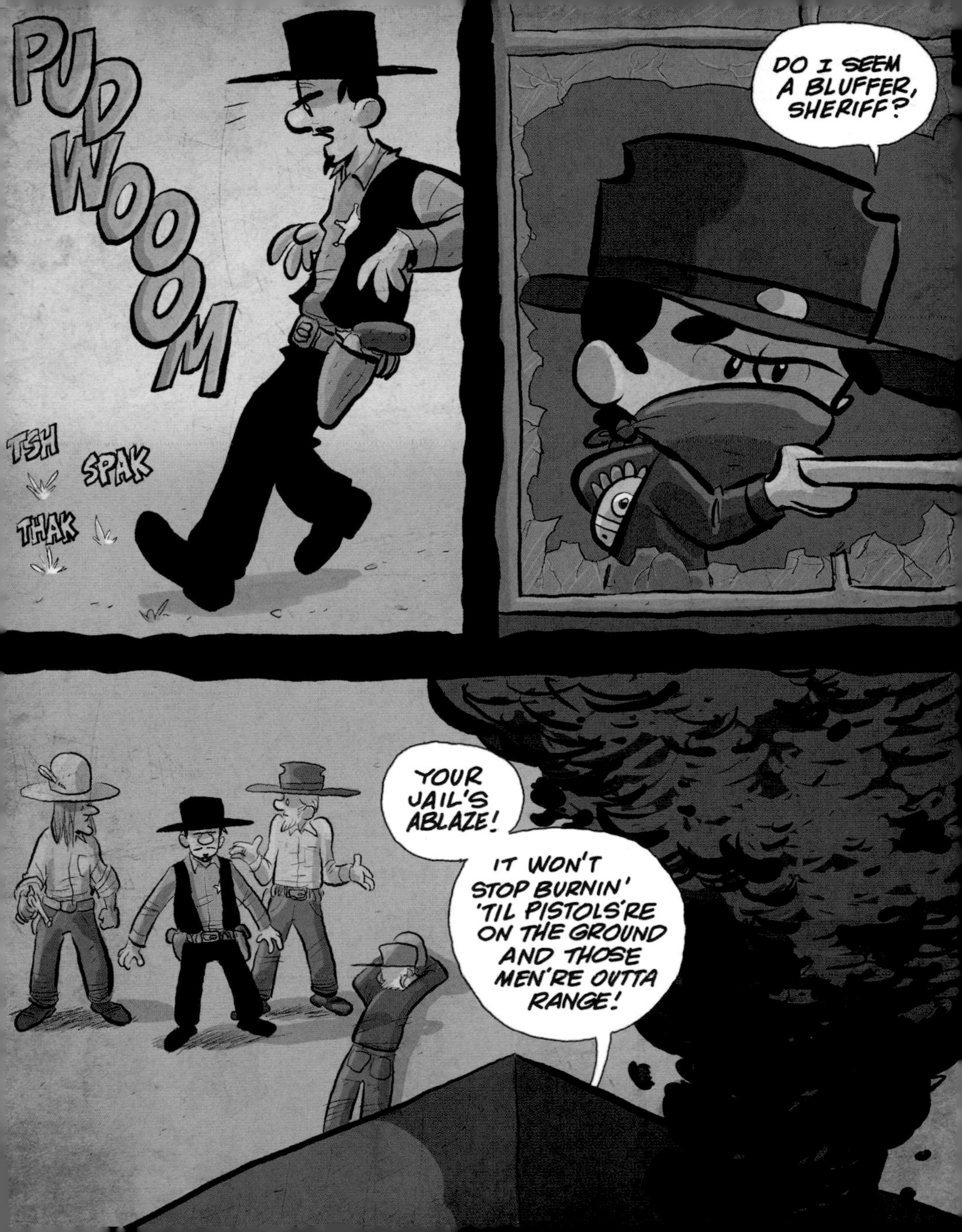
PUDWOOOOM
TSH
SPAK
THAK
DO I SEEM A BLUFFER, SHERIFF?
YOUR JAIL'S ABLAZE!
IT WON'T STOP BURNIN' 'TIL PISTOLS'RE ON THE GROUND AND THOSE MEN'RE OUTTA RANGE!

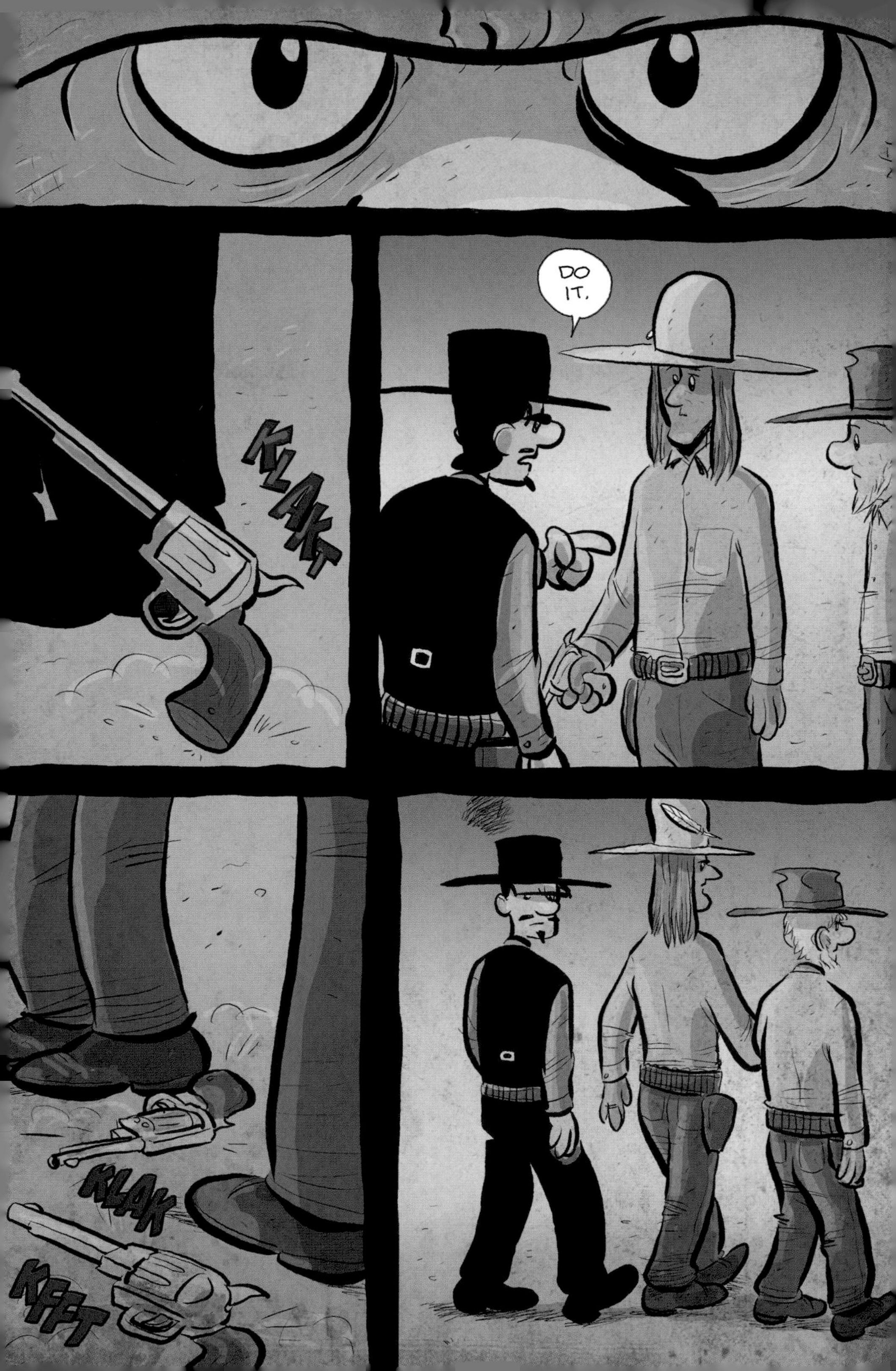
KLAKT
DO IT.
KLAK
KFFT

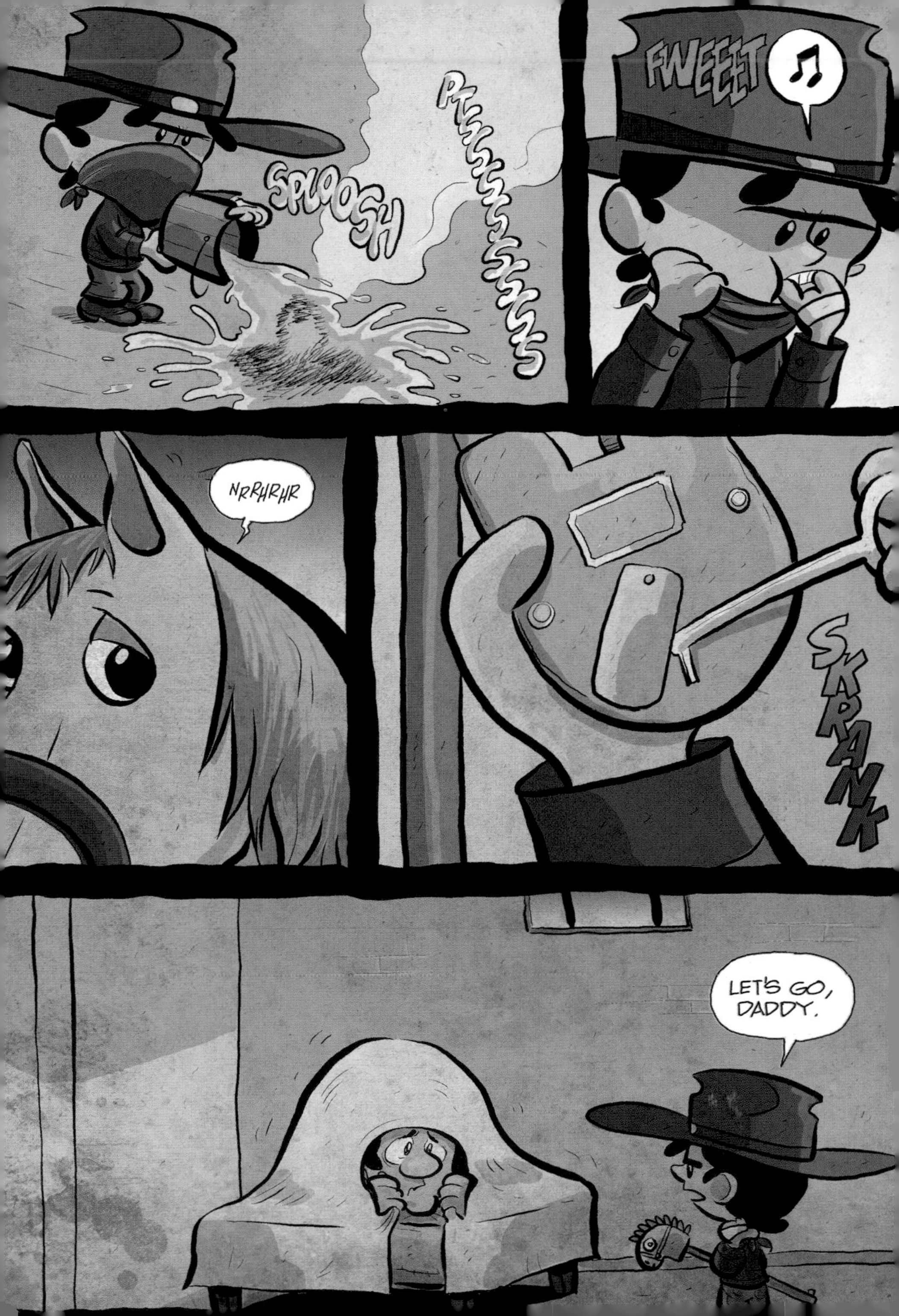
SPLOOSH
PTSSSSSSSSSS
FWEEET
♫
NRRHRHR
SKRANK
LET'S GO, DADDY.

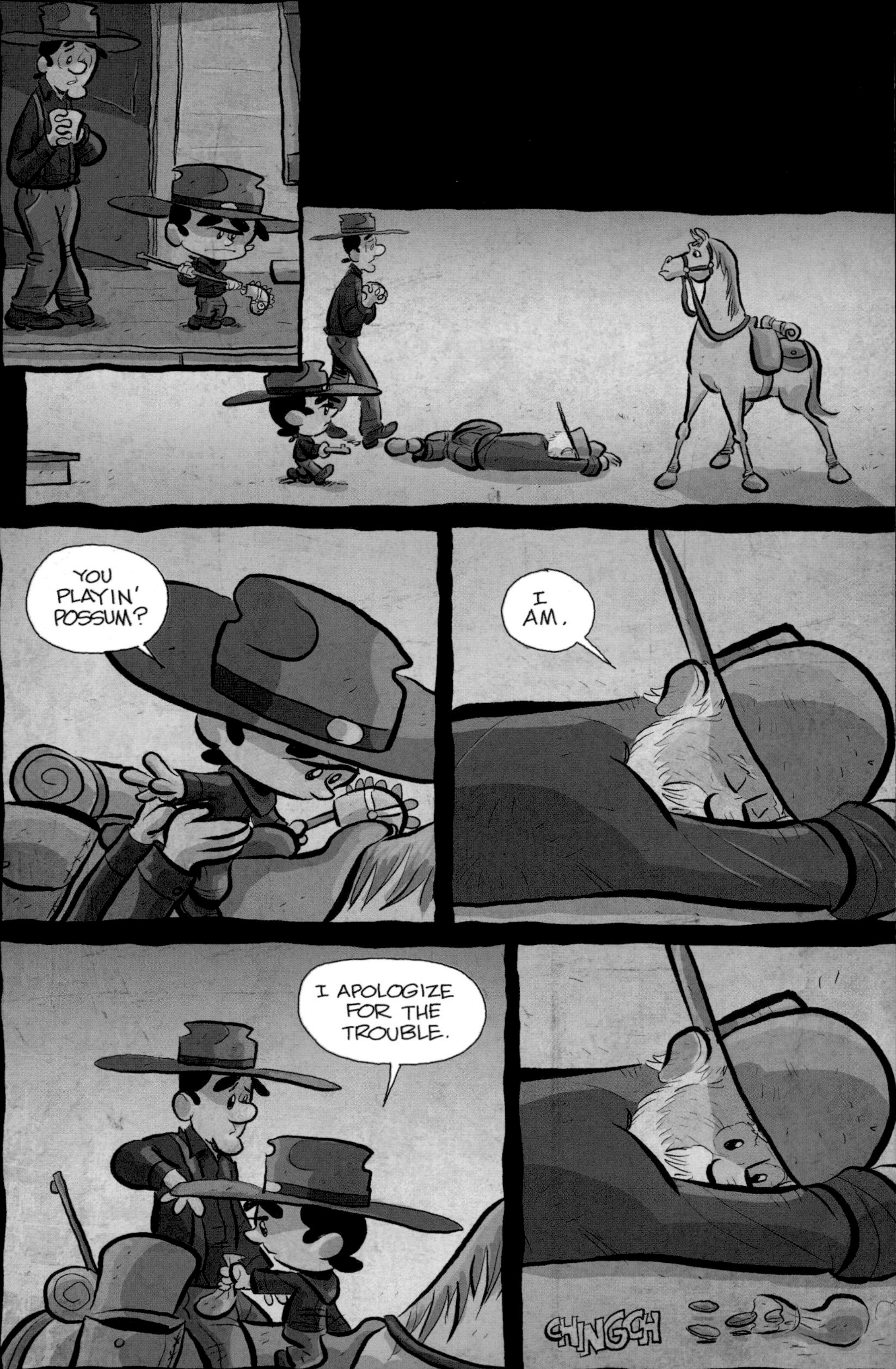
YOU PLAYIN' POSSUM?
I AM.
I APOLOGIZE FOR THE TROUBLE.
CHINGCH

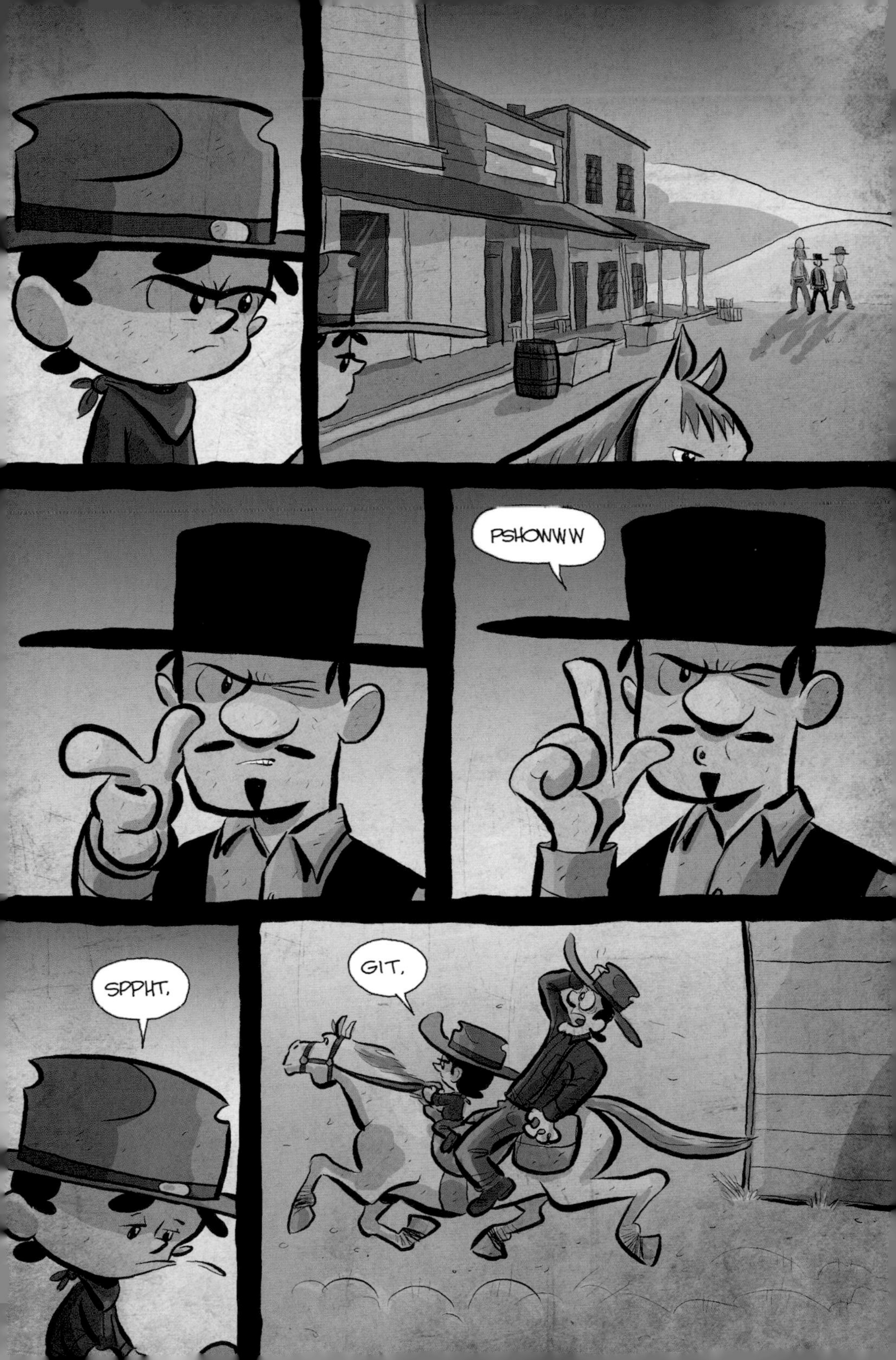
PSHOWWW
SPPHT.
GIT.

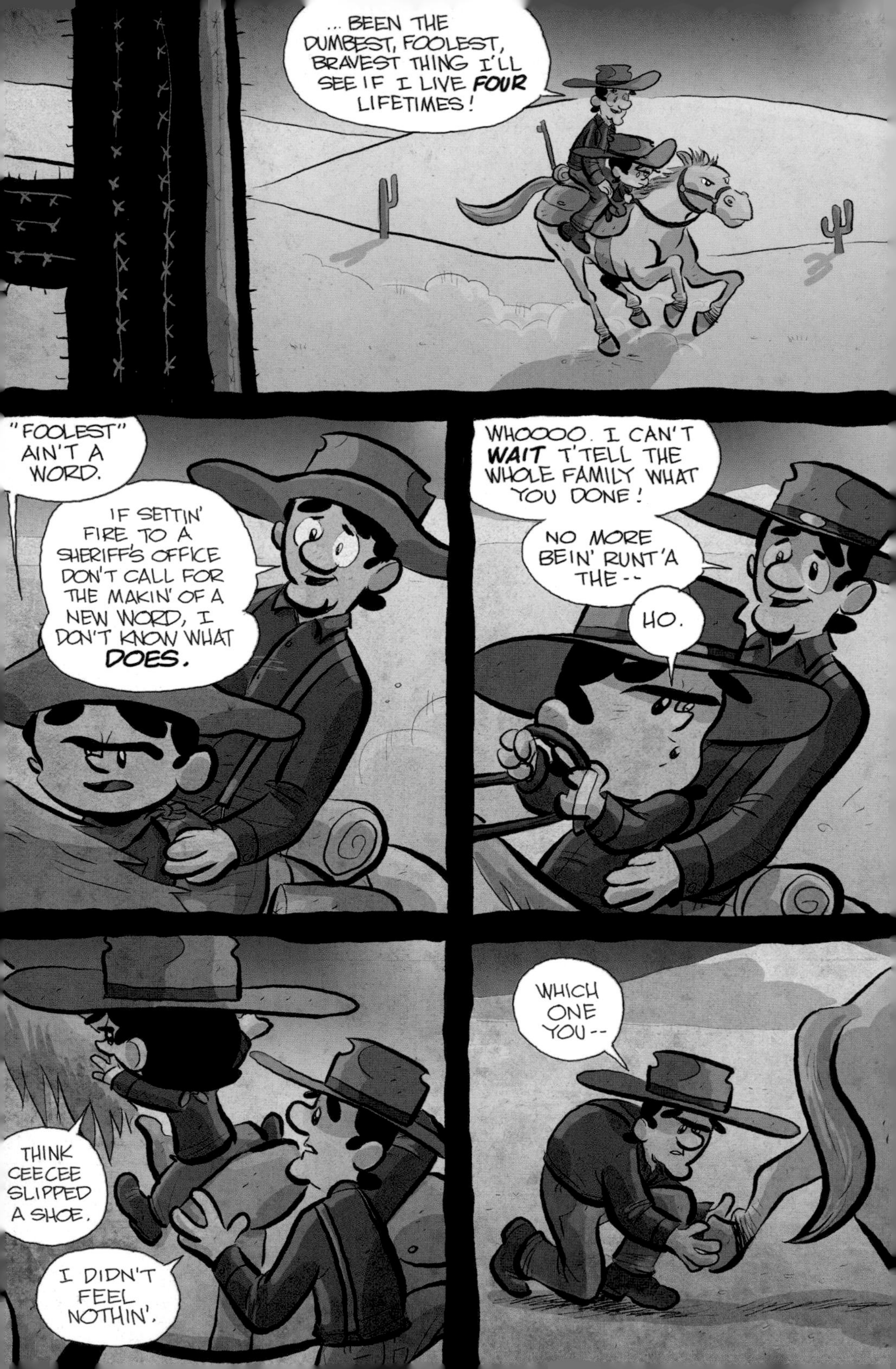

... BEEN THE DUMBEST, FOOLEST, BRAVEST THING I'LL SEE IF I LIVE **FOUR** LIFETIMES!
"FOOLEST" AIN'T A WORD.
IF SETTIN' FIRE TO A SHERIFF'S OFFICE DON'T CALL FOR THE MAKIN' OF A NEW WORD, I DON'T KNOW WHAT **DOES.**
WHOOOO. I CAN'T **WAIT** T'TELL THE WHOLE FAMILY WHAT YOU DONE!
NO MORE BEIN' RUNT'A THE--
HO.
THINK CEECEE SLIPPED A SHOE.
I DIDN'T FEEL NOTHIN'.
WHICH ONE YOU--

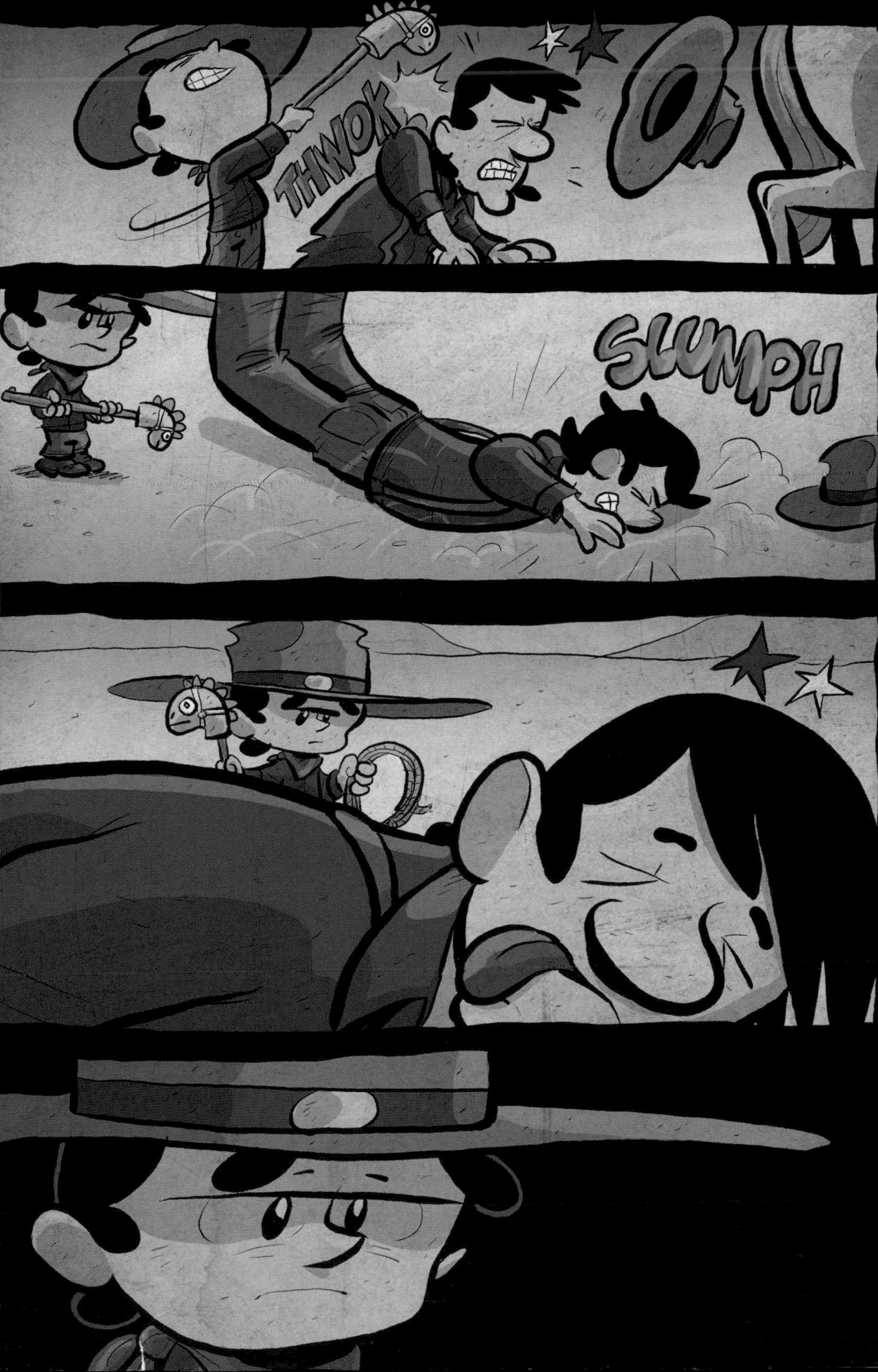
THWOK
SLUMPH

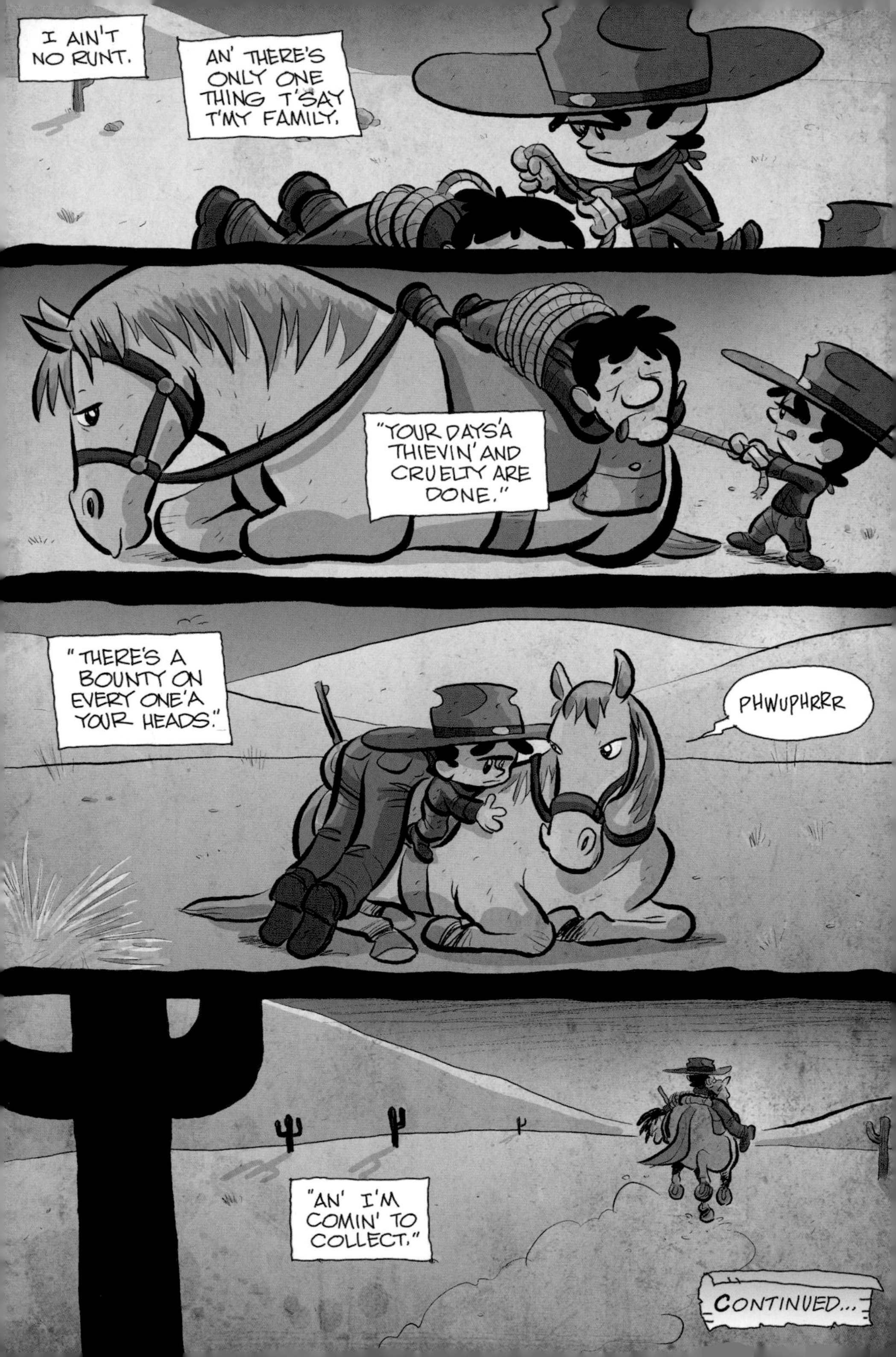
I AIN'T NO RUNT.
AN' THERE'S ONLY ONE THING T'SAY T'MY FAMILY.
"YOUR DAYS'A THIEVIN' AND CRUELTY ARE DONE."
"THERE'S A BOUNTY ON EVERY ONE'A YOUR HEADS."
PHWUPHRRR
"AN' I'M COMIN' TO COLLECT."
CONTINUED...

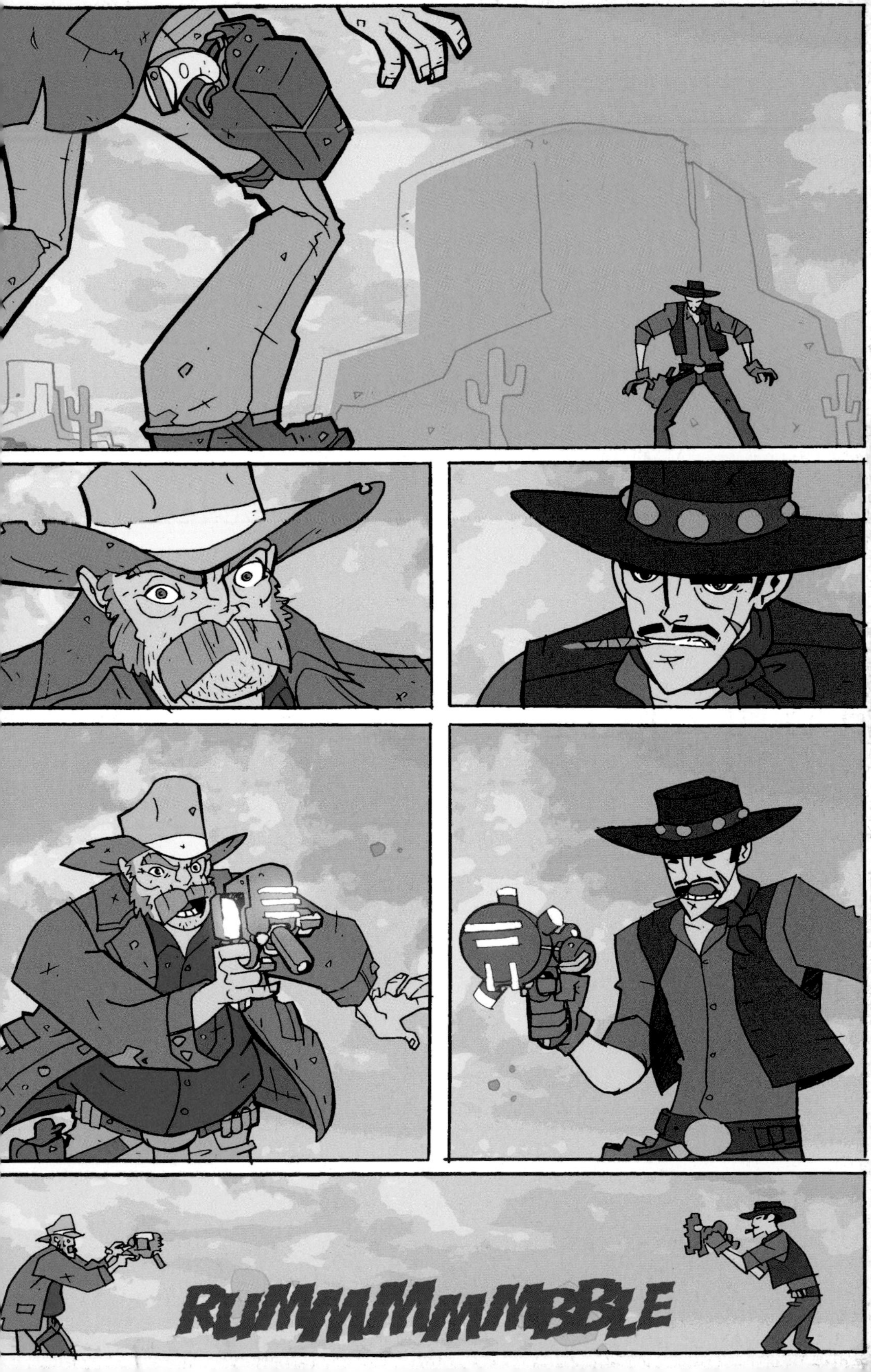
RUMMMMMMBBLE

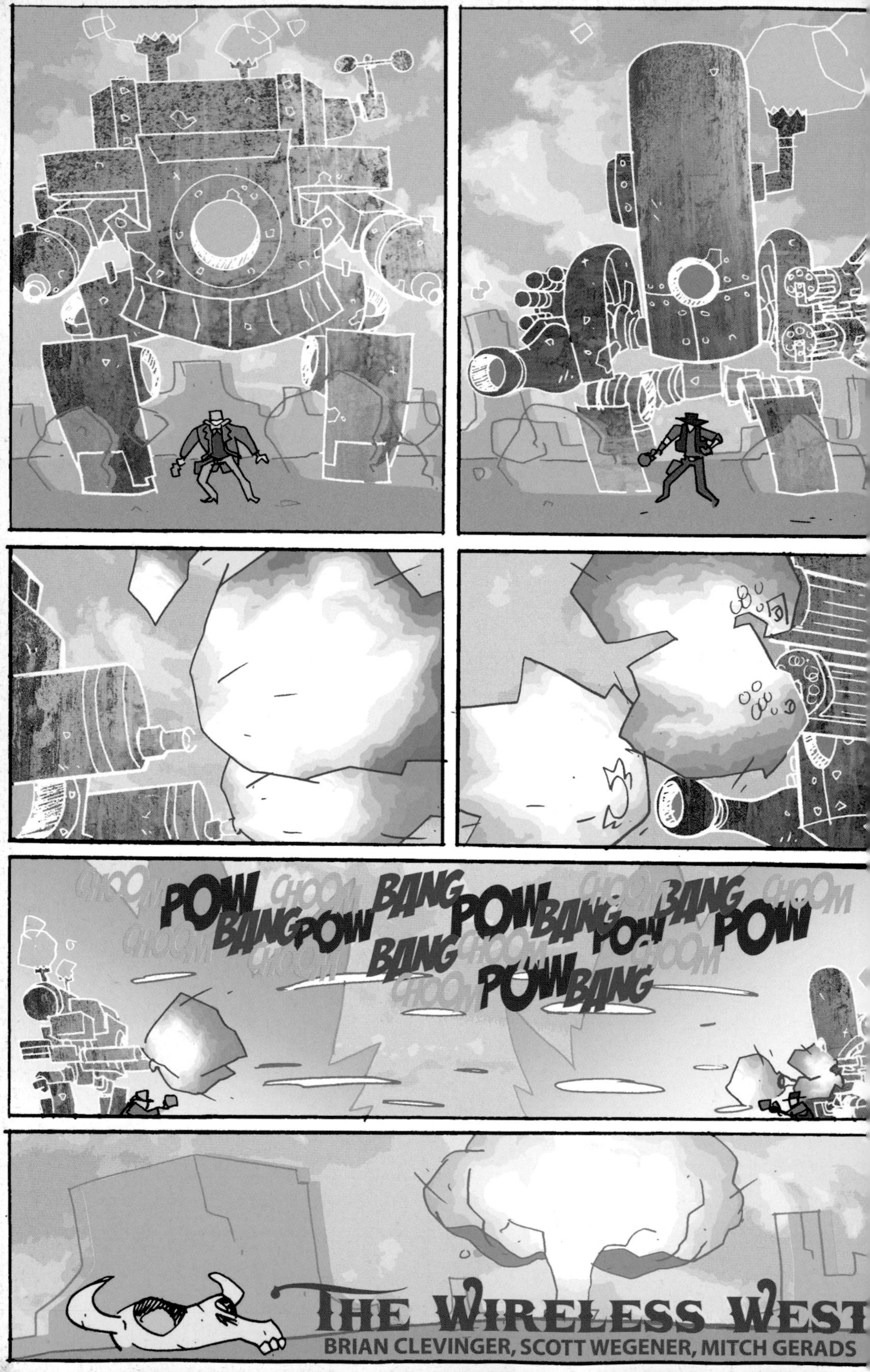
CHOOM
POW
BANG
CHOOM
POW
BANG
CHOOM
POW
BANG
BANG
CHOOM
POW
BANG
POW
CHOOM
POW
POW
BANG
THE WIRELESS WEST
BRIAN CLEVINGER, SCOTT WEGENER, MITCH GERADS

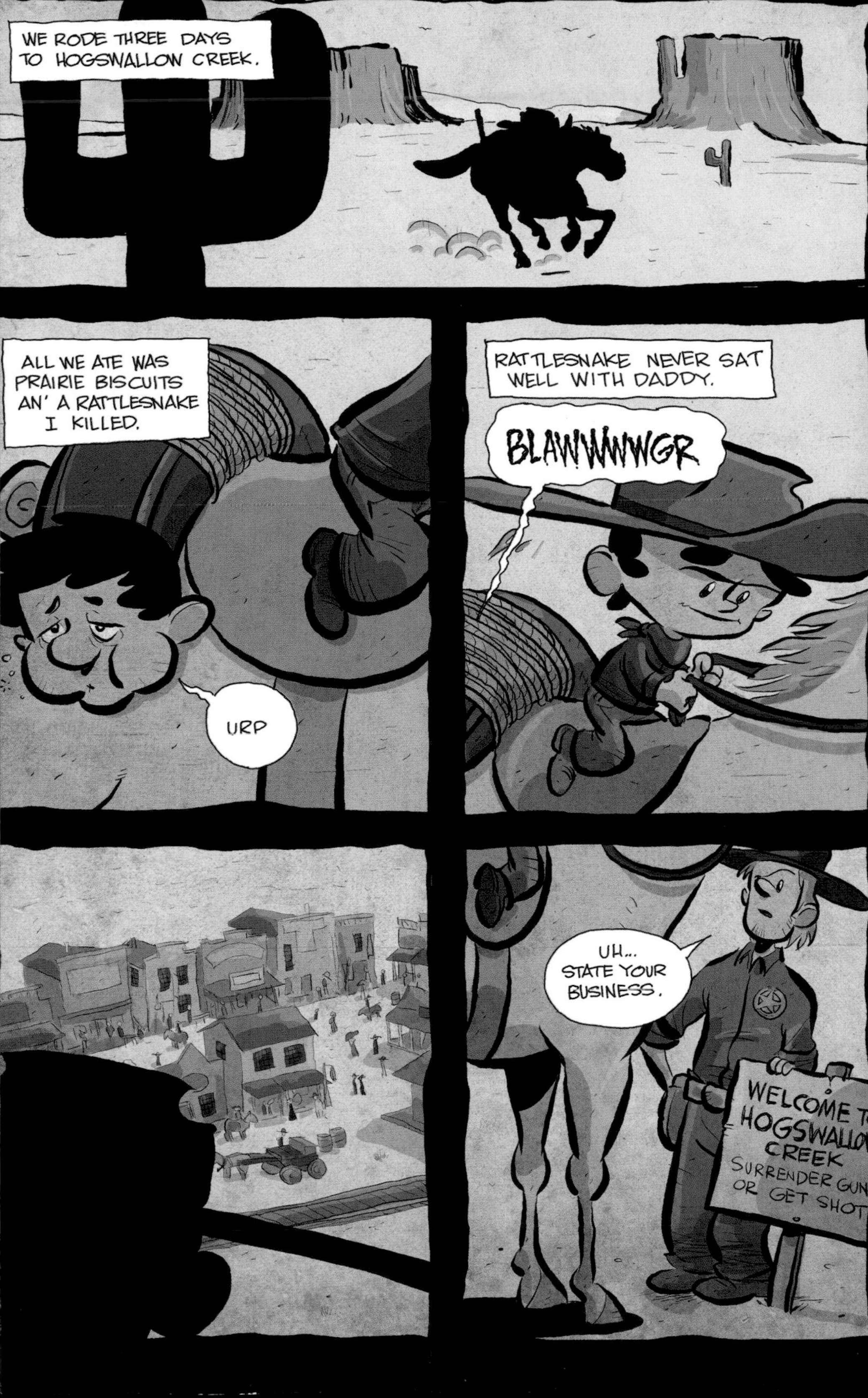
WE RODE THREE DAYS TO HOGSWALLOW CREEK.
ALL WE ATE WAS PRAIRIE BISCUITS AN' A RATTLESNAKE I KILLED.
URP
RATTLESNAKE NEVER SAT WELL WITH DADDY.
BLAWWWWGR
UH... STATE YOUR BUSINESS.
WELCOME T HOGSWALLOW CREEK
SURRENDER GUN OR GET SHOT

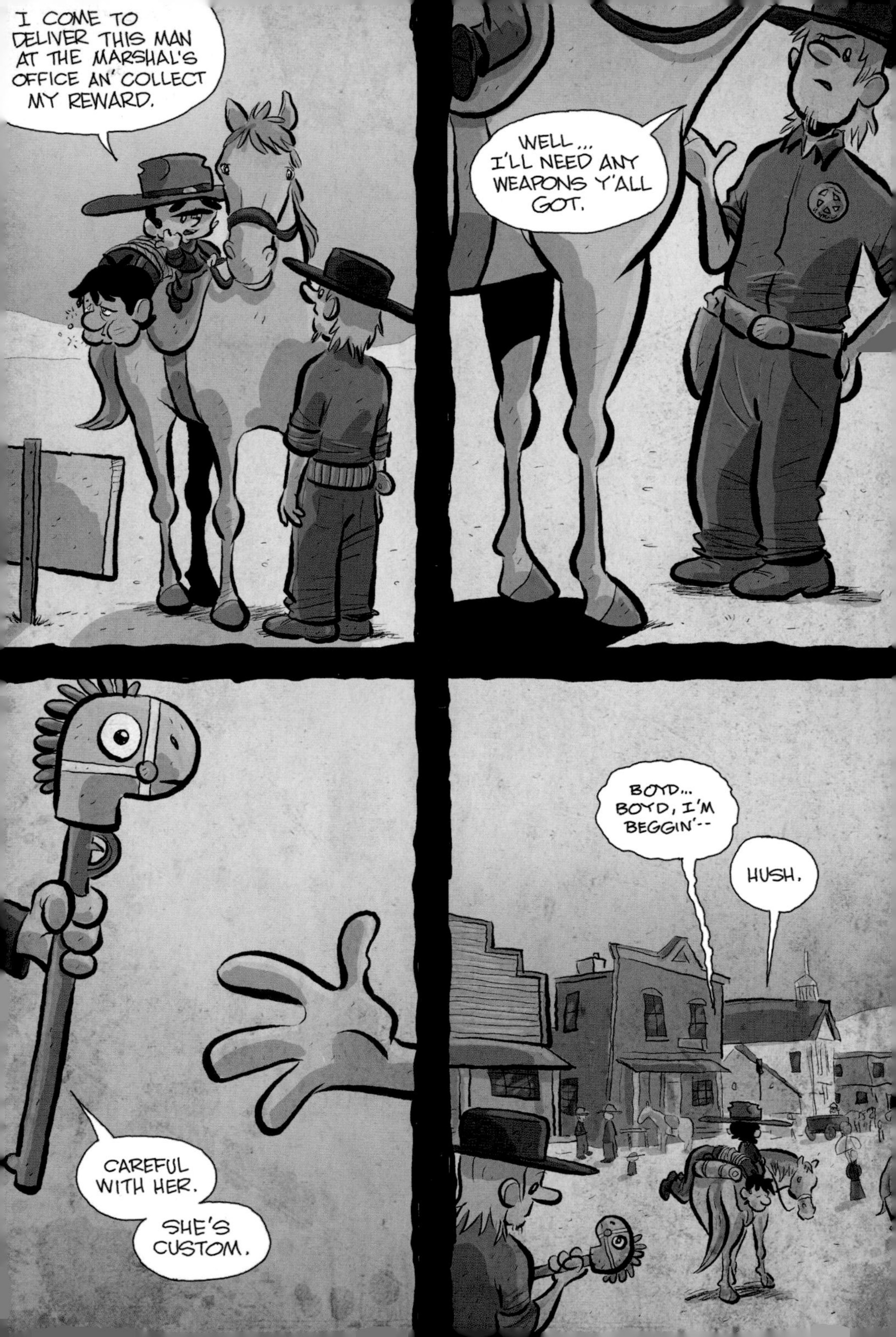
I COME TO DELIVER THIS MAN AT THE MARSHAL'S OFFICE AN' COLLECT MY REWARD.
WELL... I'LL NEED ANY WEAPONS Y'ALL GOT.
CAREFUL WITH HER.
SHE'S CUSTOM.
BOYD... BOYD, I'M BEGGIN'--
HUSH.

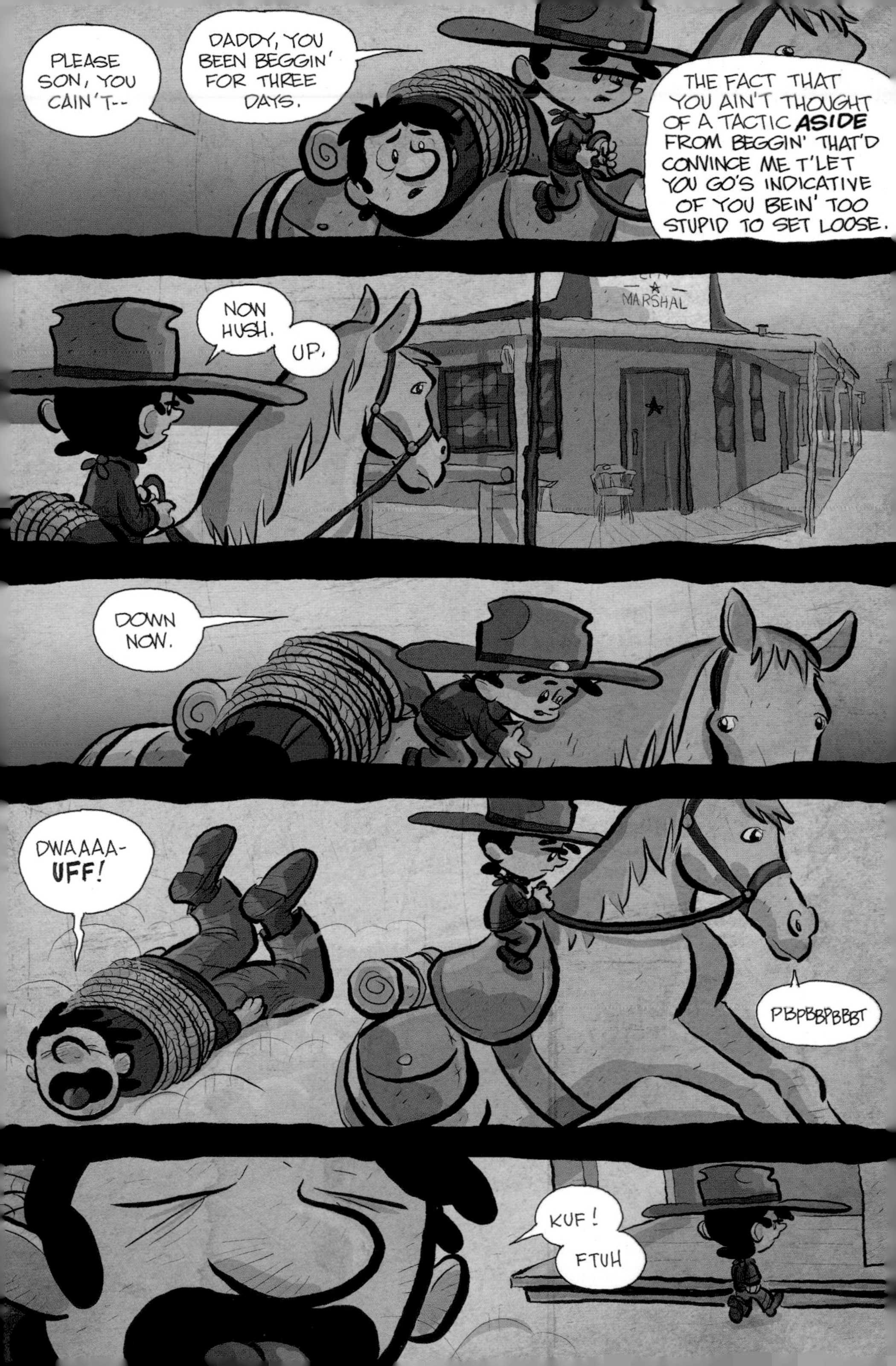
PLEASE SON, YOU CAIN'T--
DADDY, YOU BEEN BEGGIN' FOR THREE DAYS.
THE FACT THAT YOU AIN'T THOUGHT OF A TACTIC **ASIDE** FROM BEGGIN' THAT'D CONVINCE ME T'LET YOU GO'S INDICATIVE OF YOU BEIN' TOO STUPID TO SET LOOSE.
MARSHAL
NOW HUSH.
UP.
DOWN NOW.
DWAAAA-**UFF!**
PBPBBPBBBT
KUF!
FTUH

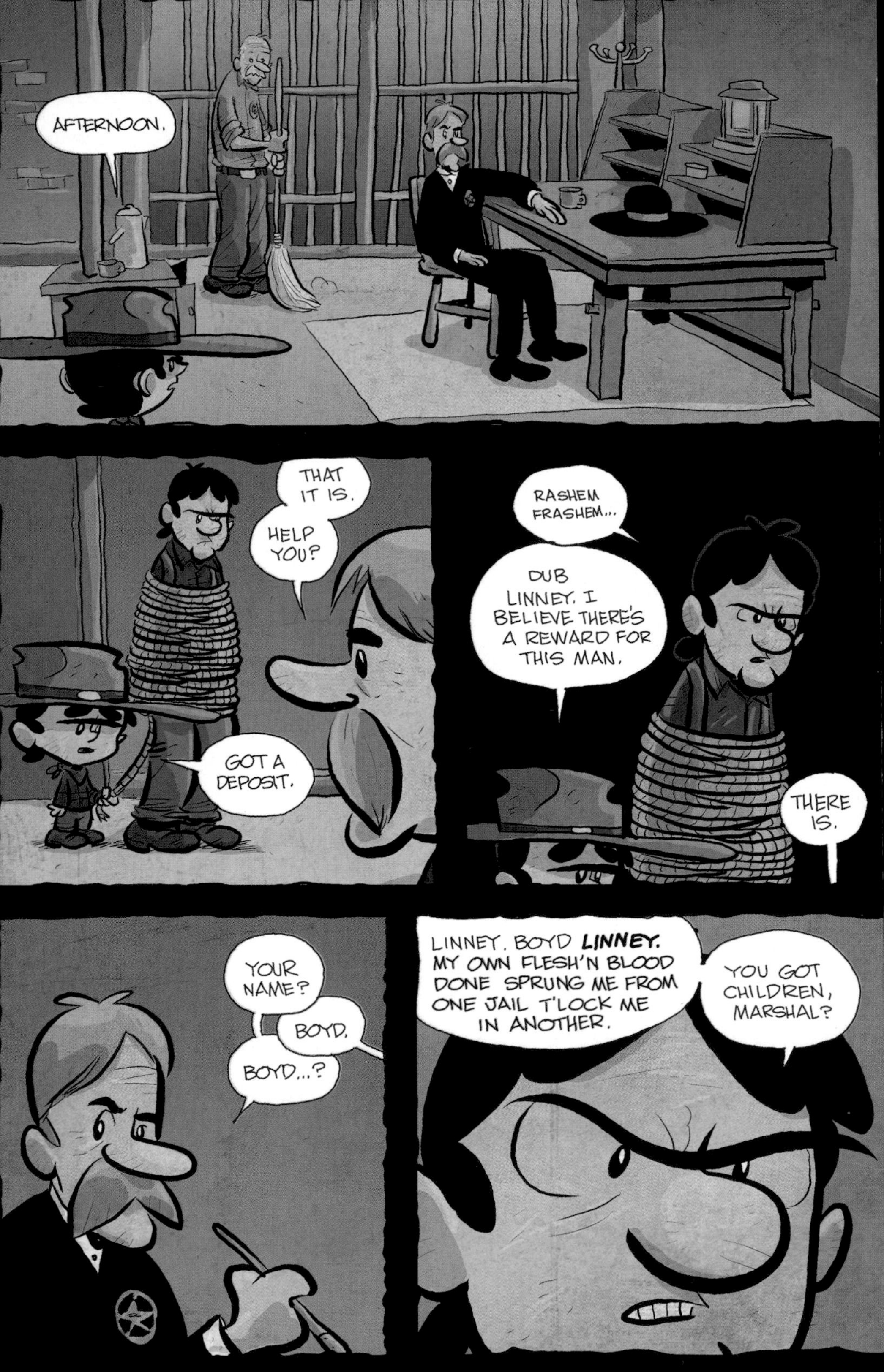
AFTERNOON.
THAT IT IS.
HELP YOU?
GOT A DEPOSIT.
RASHEM FRASHEM...
DUB LINNEY. I BELIEVE THERE'S A REWARD FOR THIS MAN.
THERE IS.
YOUR NAME?
BOYD.
BOYD...?
LINNEY. BOYD **LINNEY.** MY OWN FLESH'N BLOOD DONE SPRUNG ME FROM ONE JAIL T'LOCK ME IN ANOTHER.
YOU GOT CHILDREN, MARSHAL?

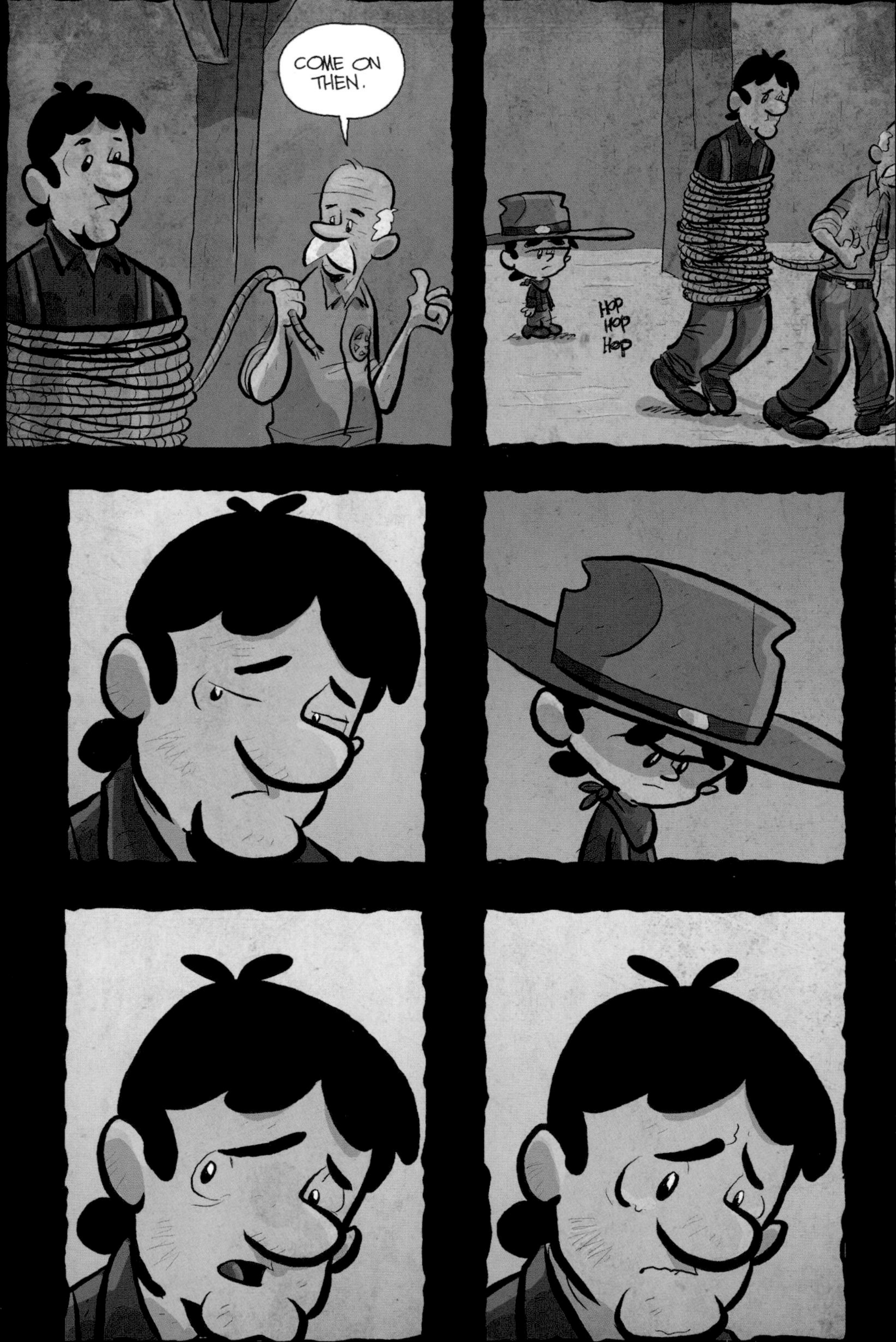
COME ON THEN.
HOP HOP HOP

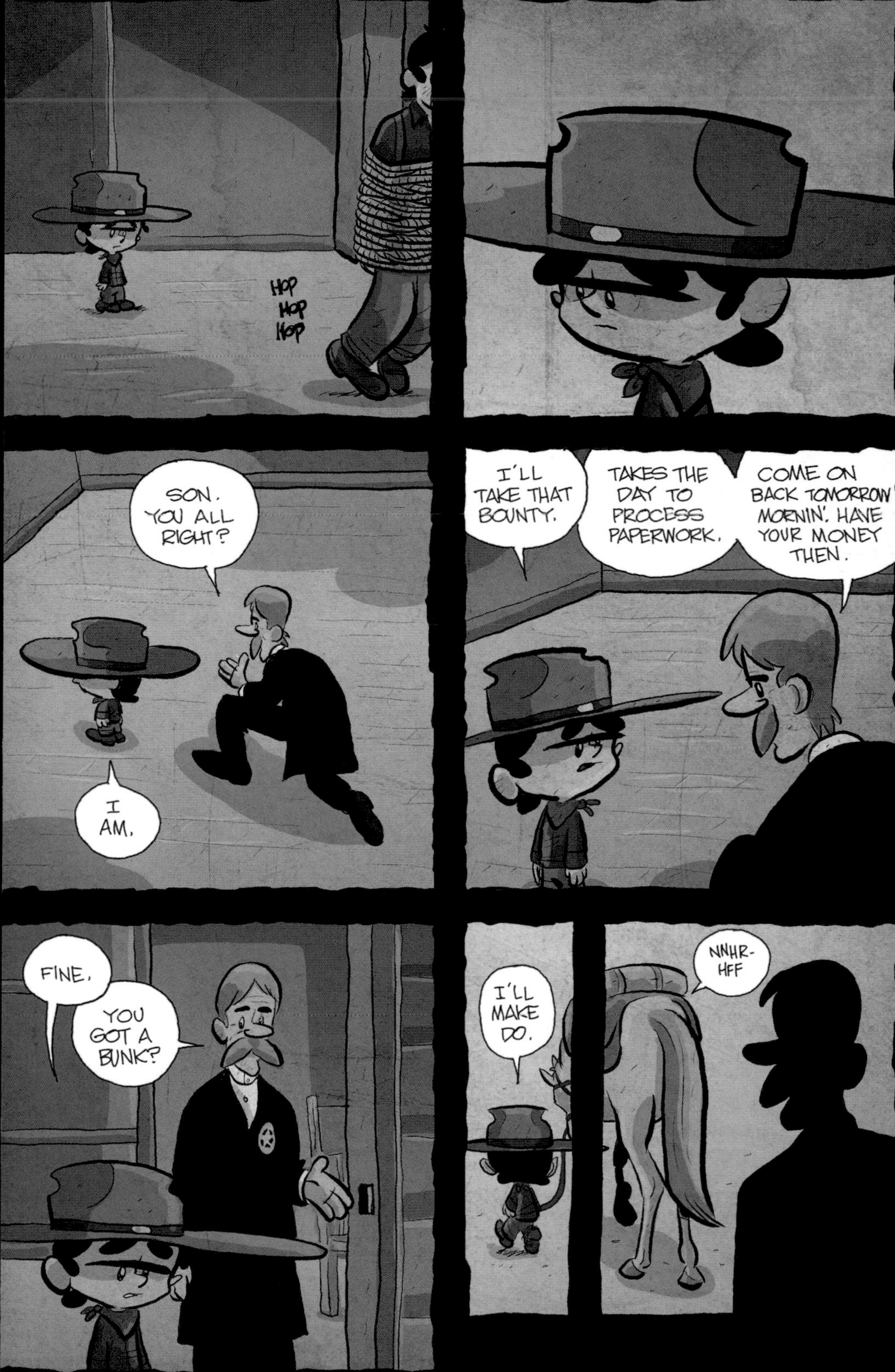
HOP
HOP
HOP
SON. YOU ALL RIGHT?
I AM.
I'LL TAKE THAT BOUNTY.
TAKES THE DAY TO PROCESS PAPERWORK.
COME ON BACK TOMORROW MORNIN'. HAVE YOUR MONEY THEN.
FINE.
YOU GOT A BUNK?
I'LL MAKE DO.
NNHR-HFF

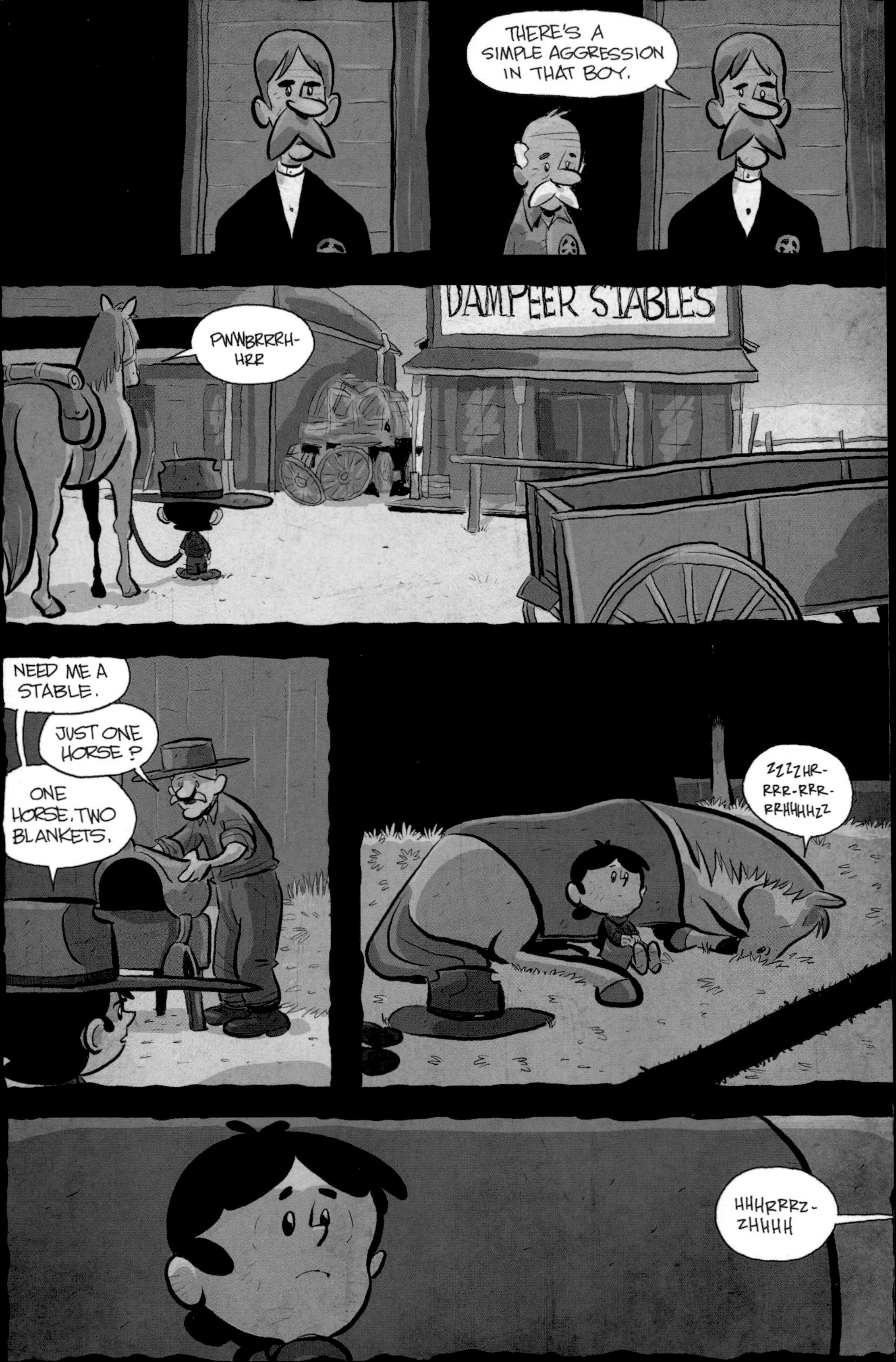
THERE'S A SIMPLE AGGRESSION IN THAT BOY.
DAMPEER STABLES
PWWBRRRH-HRR
NEED ME A STABLE.
JUST ONE HORSE?
ONE HORSE, TWO BLANKETS.
ZZZZHR-RRR-RRR-RRHHHHZZ
HHHRRRZ-ZHHHH

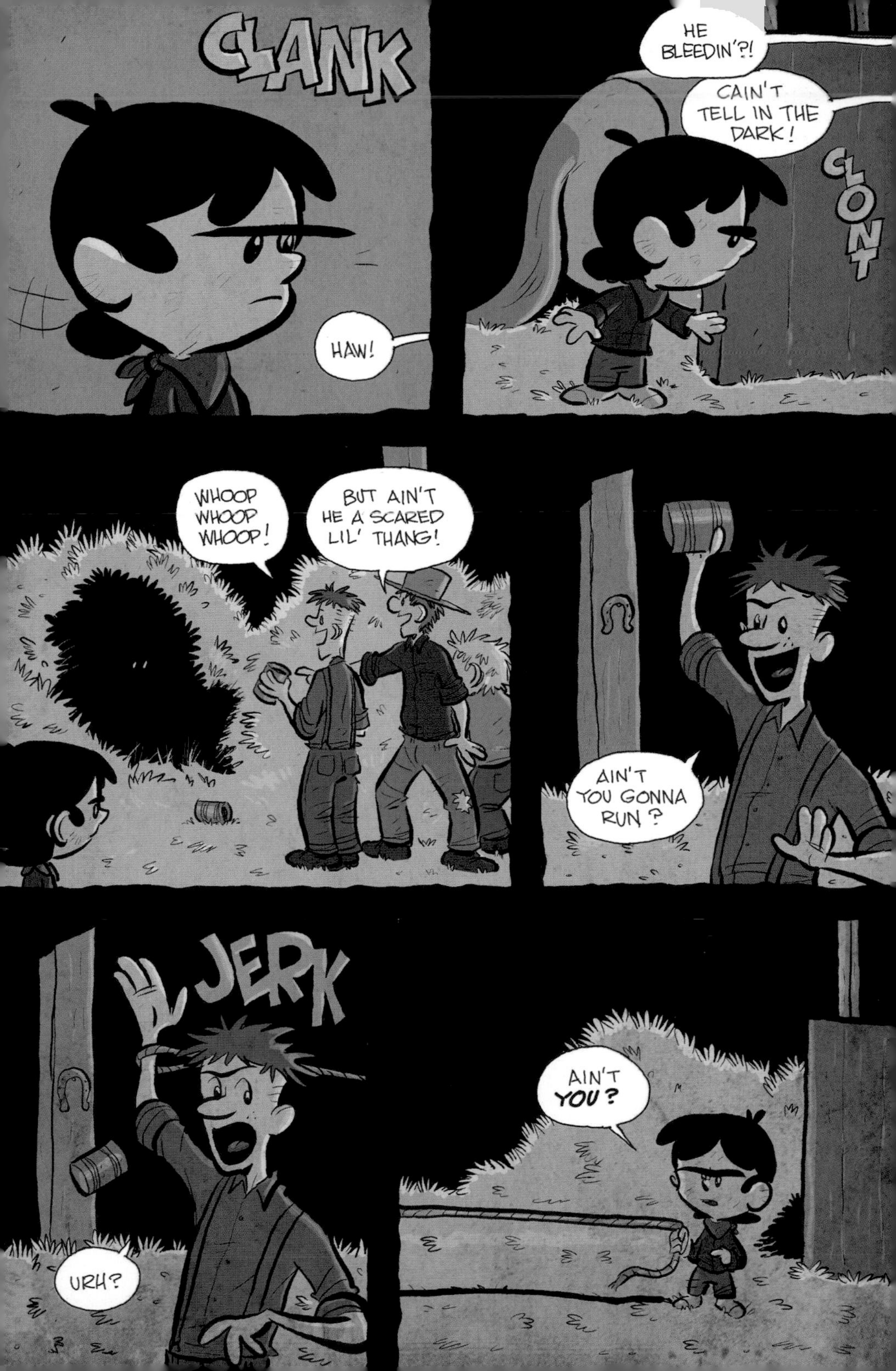
CLANK
HAW!
HE BLEEDIN'?!
CAIN'T TELL IN THE DARK!
CLONT
WHOOP WHOOP WHOOP!
BUT AIN'T HE A SCARED LIL' THANG!
AIN'T YOU GONNA RUN?
JERK
URH?
AIN'T YOU?

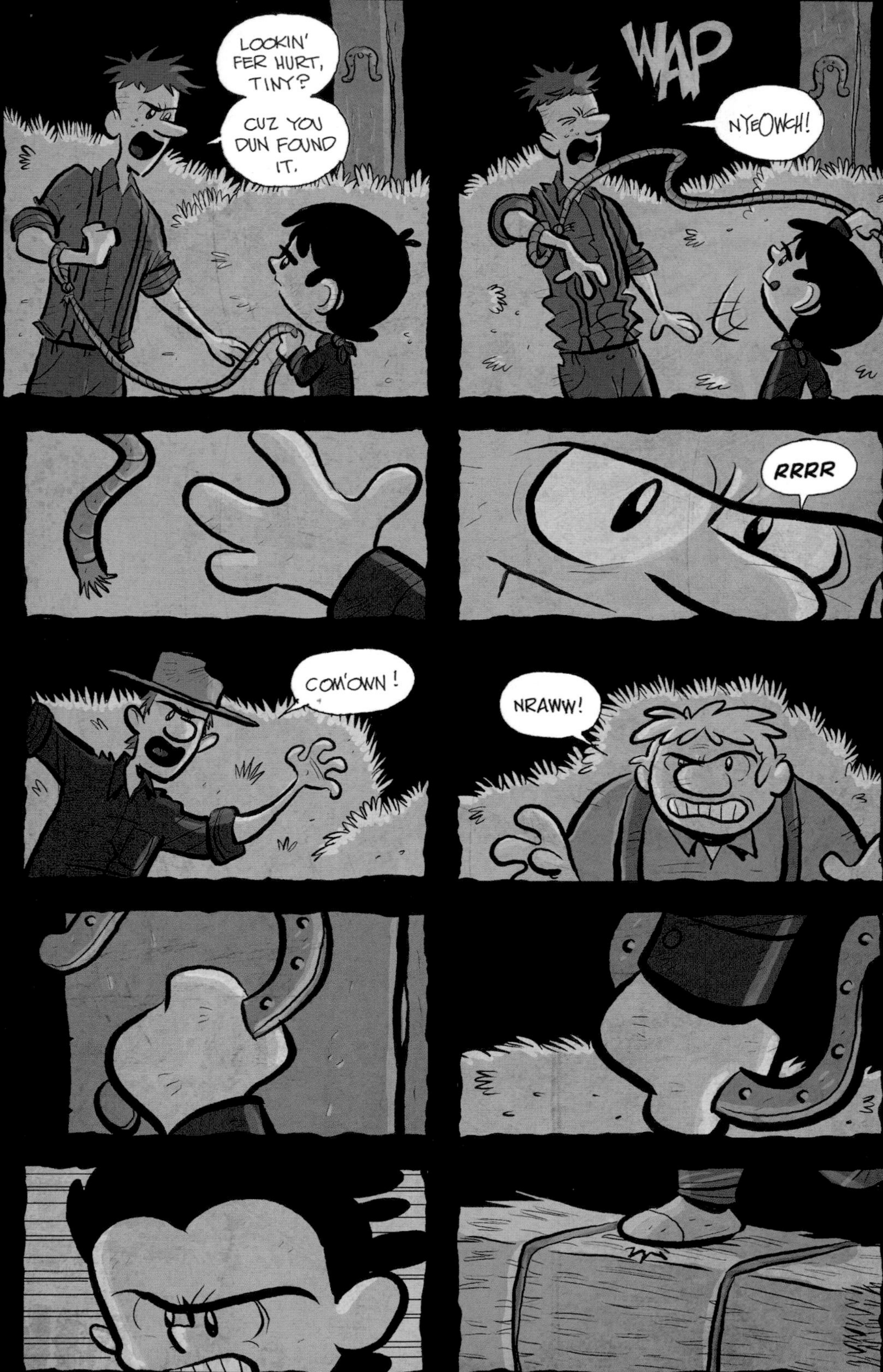
LOOKIN' FER HURT, TINY?
CUZ YOU DUN FOUND IT.
WAP
NYEOWCH!
RRRR
COM'OWN!
NRAWW!

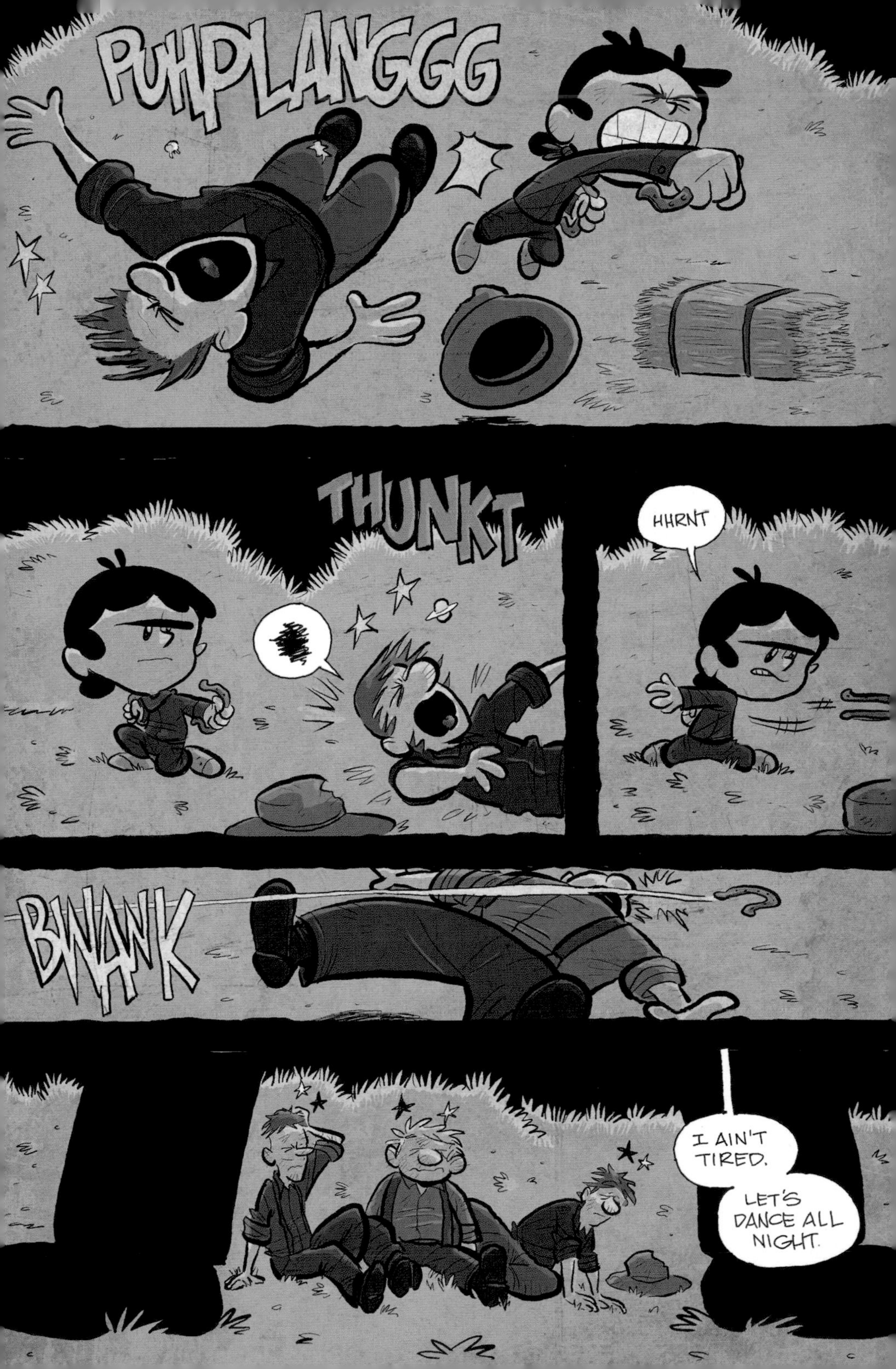
PUHPLANGGG
THUNKT
HHRNT
BWANK
I AIN'T TIRED.
LET'S DANCE ALL NIGHT.

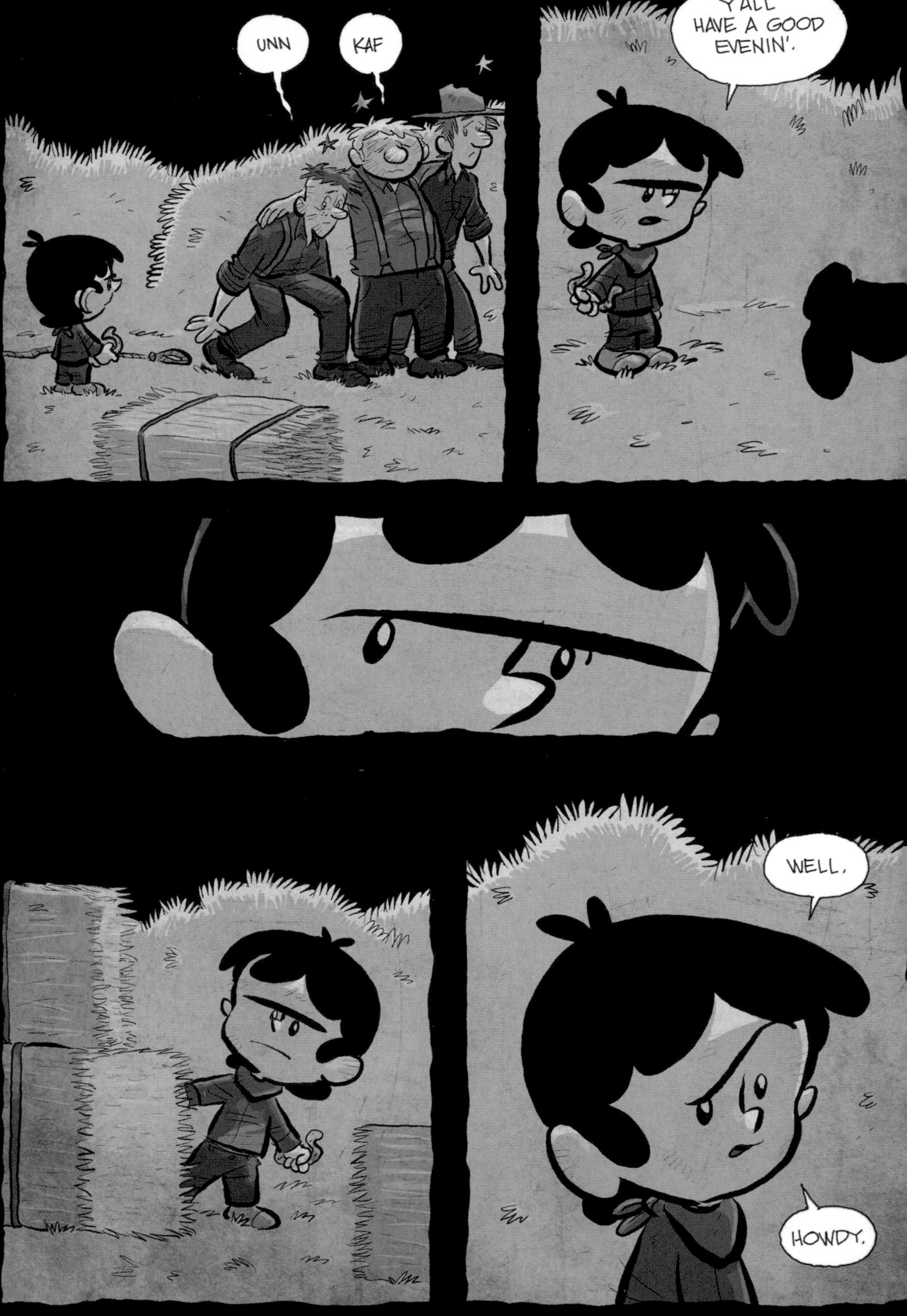
UNN
KAF
Y'ALL HAVE A GOOD EVENIN'.
WELL.
HOWDY.

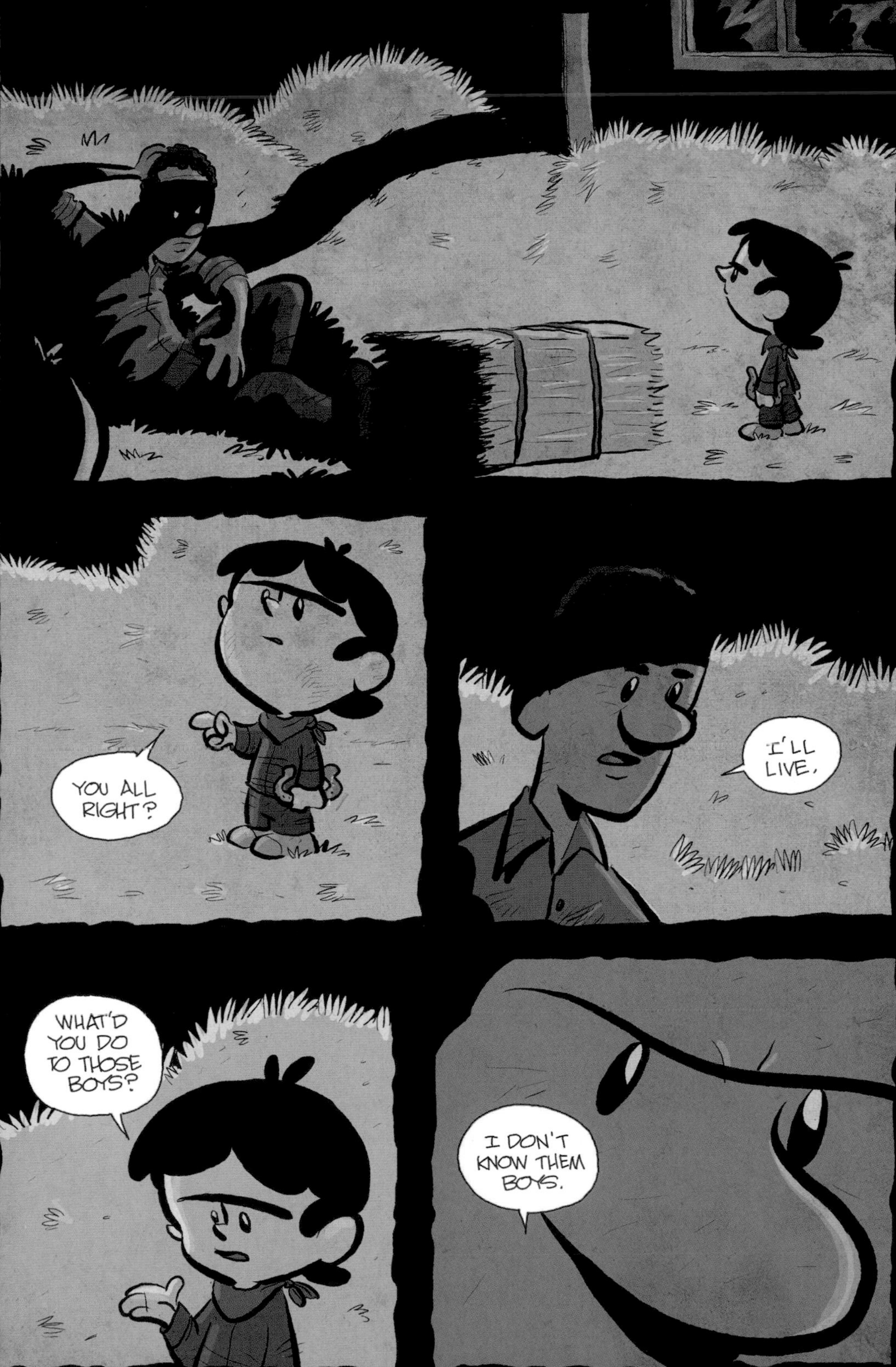
YOU ALL RIGHT?
I'LL LIVE.
WHAT'D YOU DO TO THOSE BOYS?
I DON'T KNOW THEM BOYS.

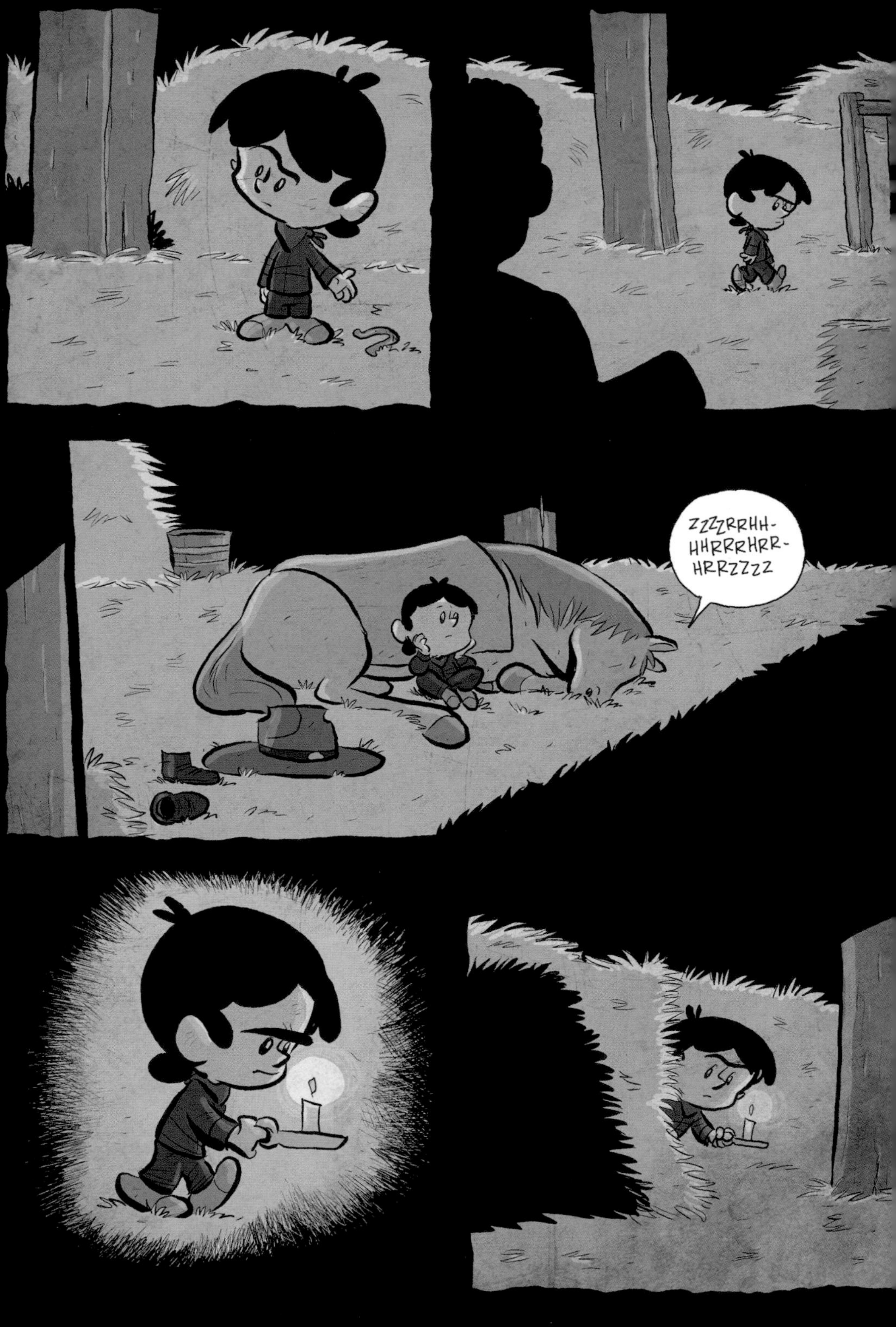
ZZZZRRHH-HHRRRHRR-HRRZZZZ

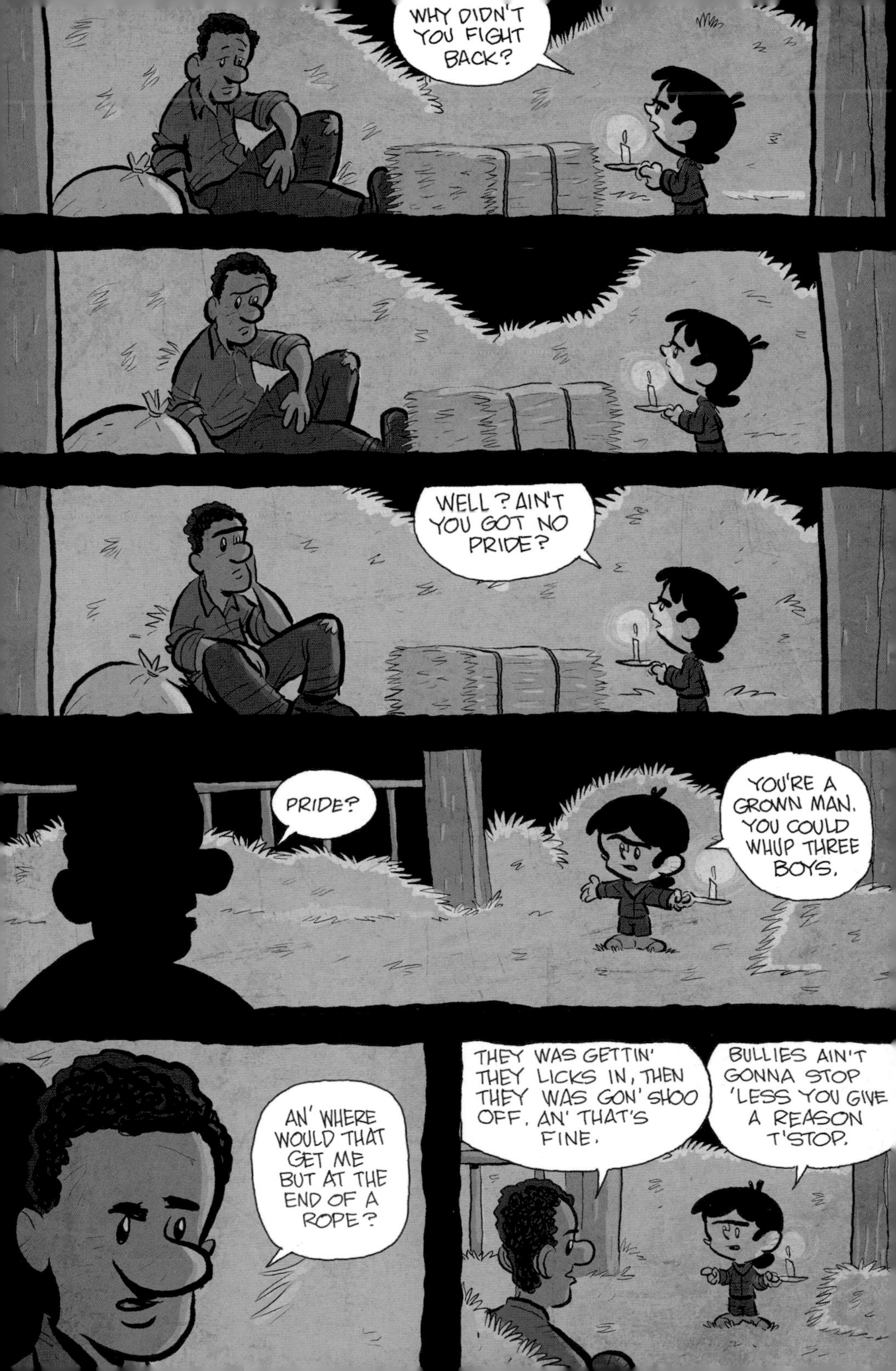
WHY DIDN'T YOU FIGHT BACK?
WELL? AIN'T YOU GOT NO PRIDE?
PRIDE?
YOU'RE A GROWN MAN. YOU COULD WHUP THREE BOYS.
AN' WHERE WOULD THAT GET ME BUT AT THE END OF A ROPE?
THEY WAS GETTIN' THEY LICKS IN, THEN THEY WAS GON' SHOO OFF. AN' THAT'S FINE.
BULLIES AIN'T GONNA STOP 'LESS YOU GIVE A REASON T'STOP.

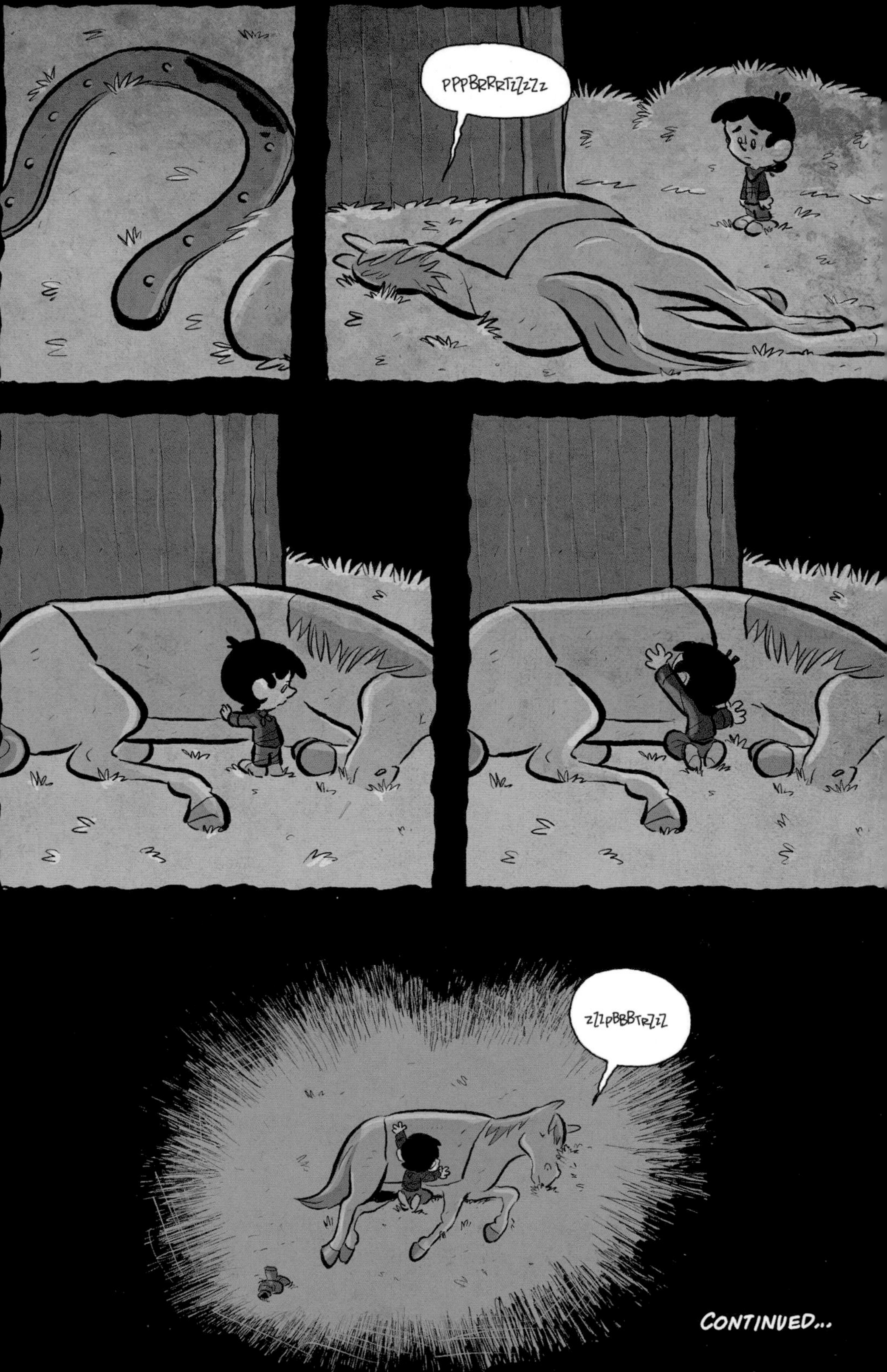
PPPBRRRTZZZZZ
ZZZPBBBTRZZZ
CONTINUED...

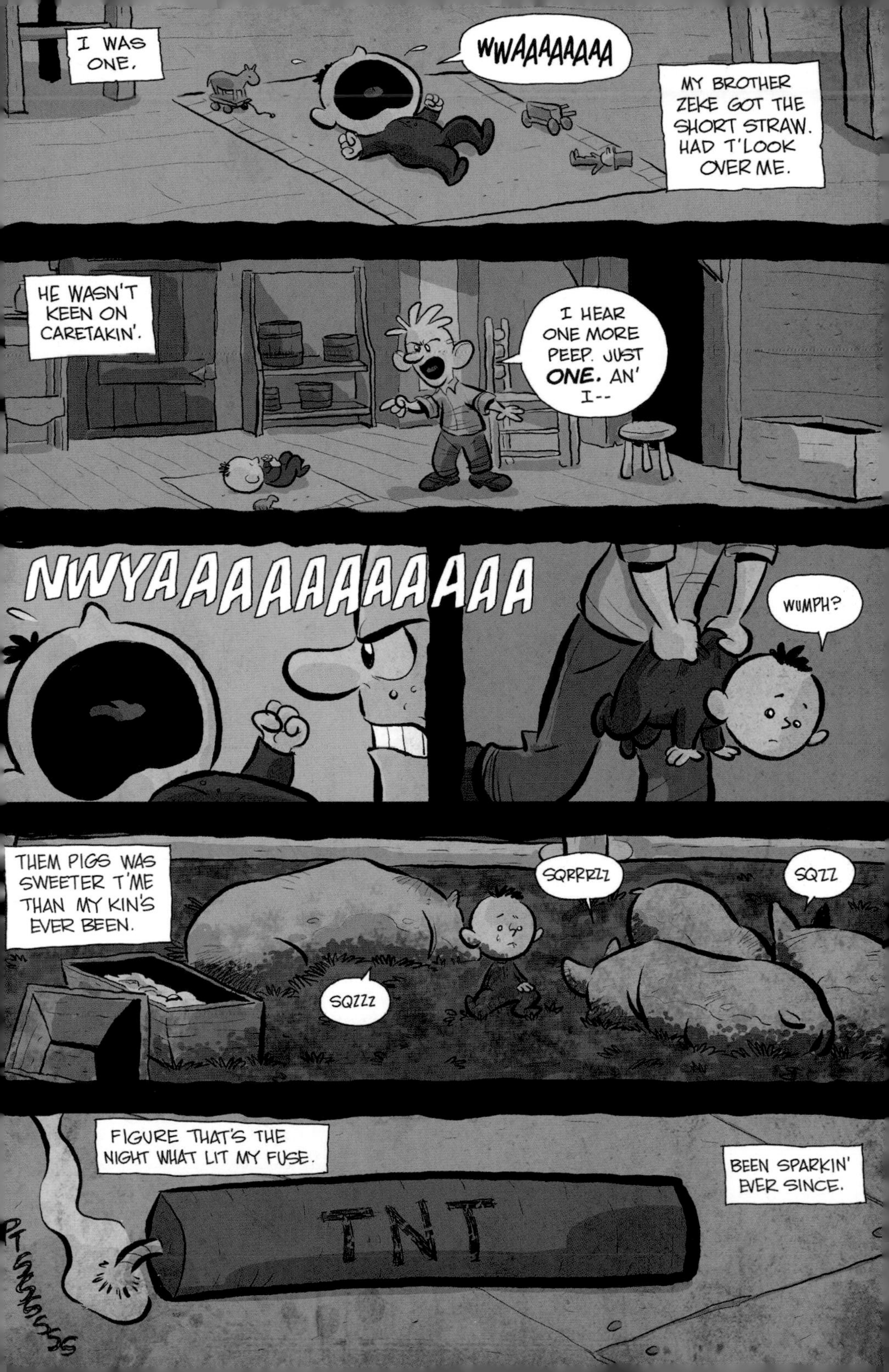
I WAS ONE.
WWAAAAAAAA
MY BROTHER ZEKE GOT THE SHORT STRAW. HAD T'LOOK OVER ME.
HE WASN'T KEEN ON CARETAKIN'.
I HEAR ONE MORE PEEP. JUST **ONE.** AN' I--
NWYAAAAAAAAAAA
WUMPH?
THEM PIGS WAS SWEETER T'ME THAN MY KIN'S EVER BEEN.
SQRRRZZ
SQZZ
SQZZZ
FIGURE THAT'S THE NIGHT WHAT LIT MY FUSE.
BEEN SPARKIN' EVER SINCE.
TNT
PTSSSSSSSS

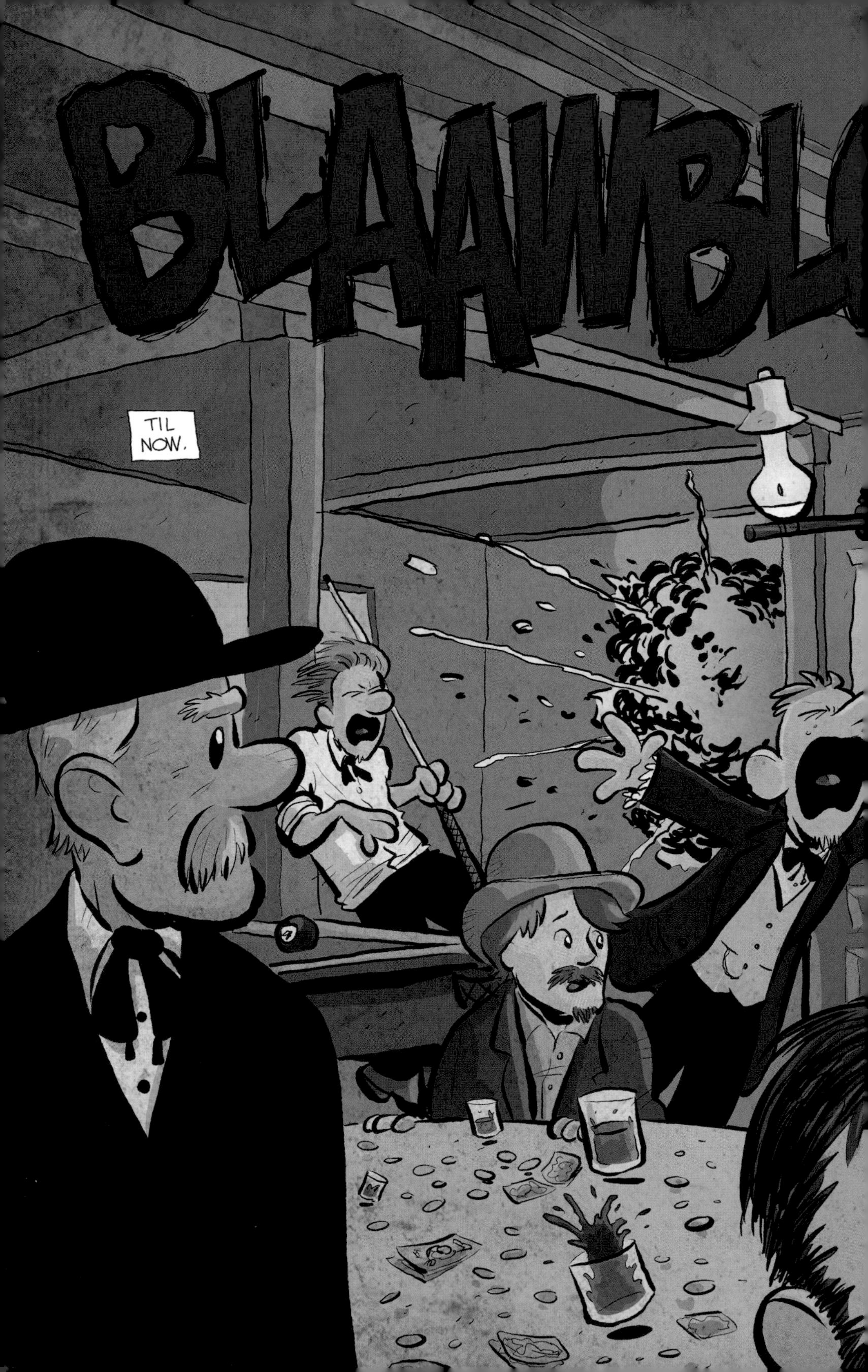
BLAAWBL
TIL NOW.

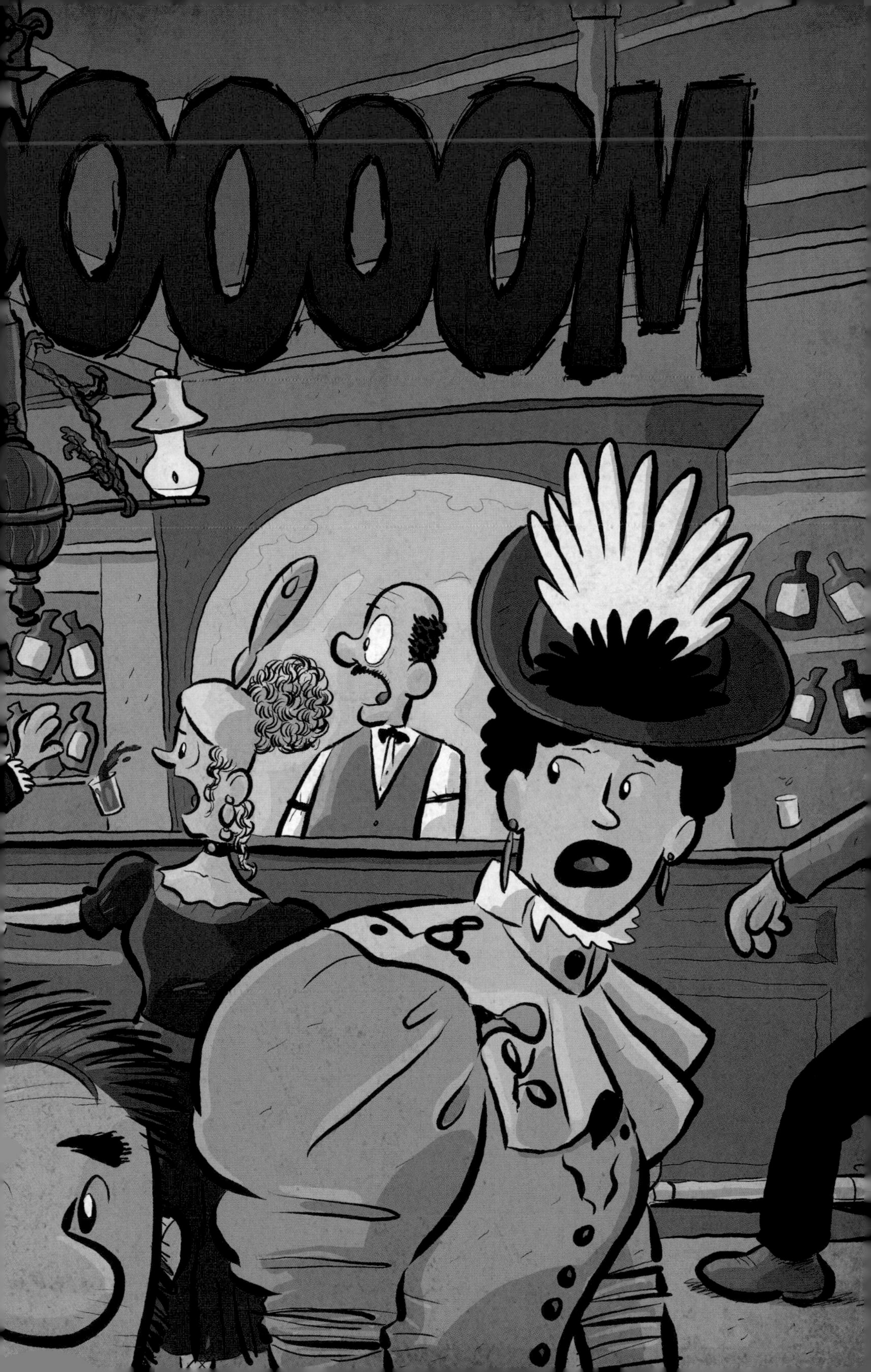
OOOOM

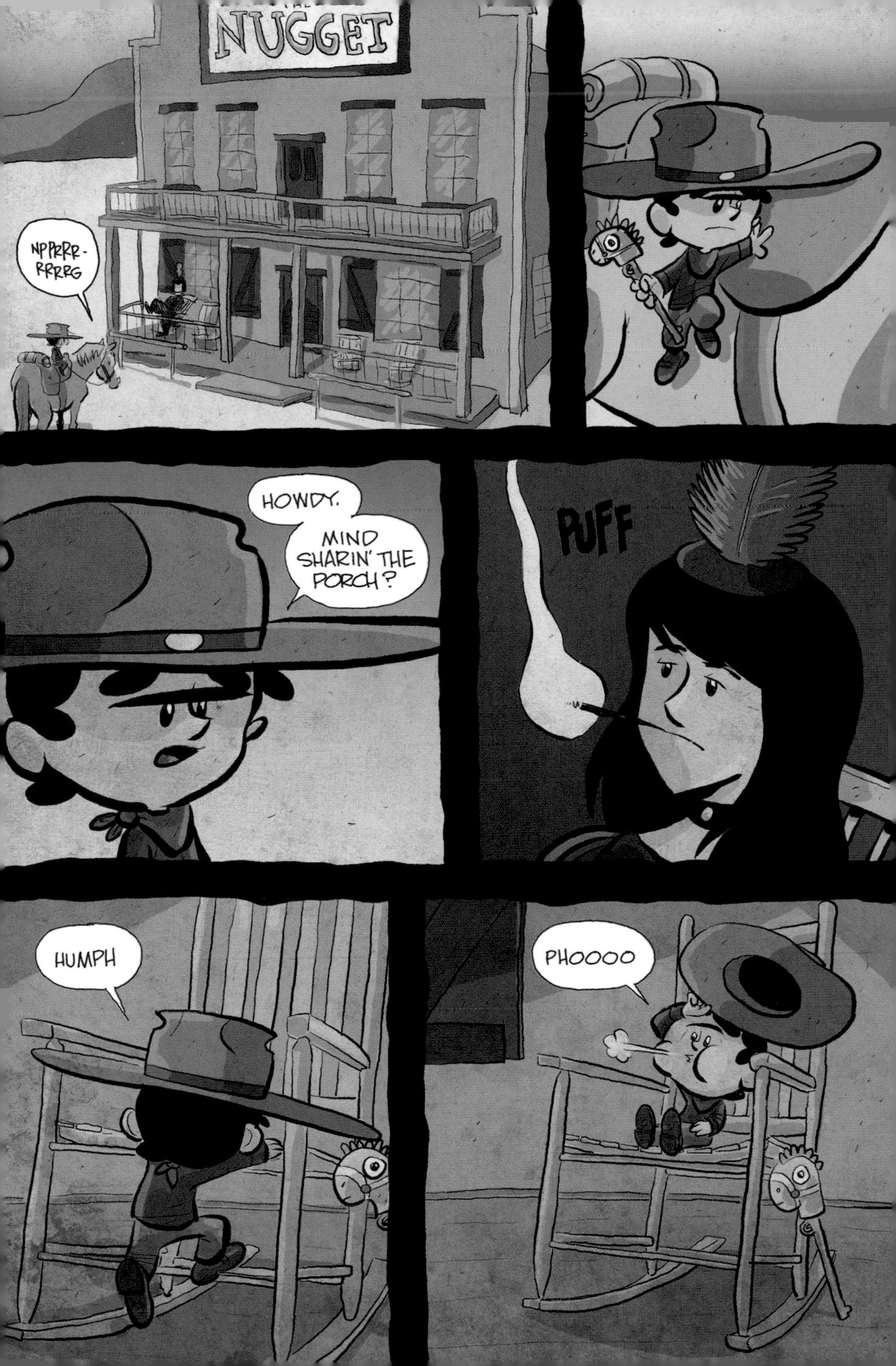
NUGGET
NPPRRR-RRRRG
HOWDY.
MIND SHARIN' THE PORCH?
PUFF
HUMPH
PHOOOO

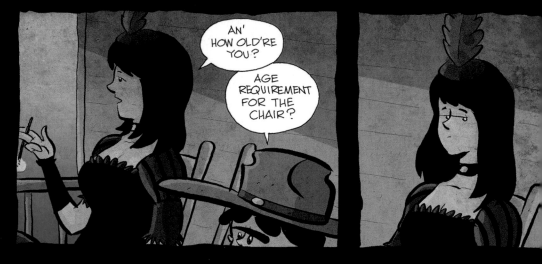

AN' HOW OLD'RE YOU?

AGE REQUIREMENT FOR THE CHAIR?

TEN.

FAIRLY MATURE FOR MY AGE.

CRKK

MM.

MATURE ENOUGH FOR A DEADLY WEAPON.

IT AIN'T NO GUN.

JUST A PEASHOOTER WITH A LOUD HOLLER.

KRNIK

YOU INTEND TO CAUSE A RUCKUS?

I DO NOT.

BUT THE BYPRODUCT OF MY INTENTIONS COULD WELL LEAD TO RUCKUS.

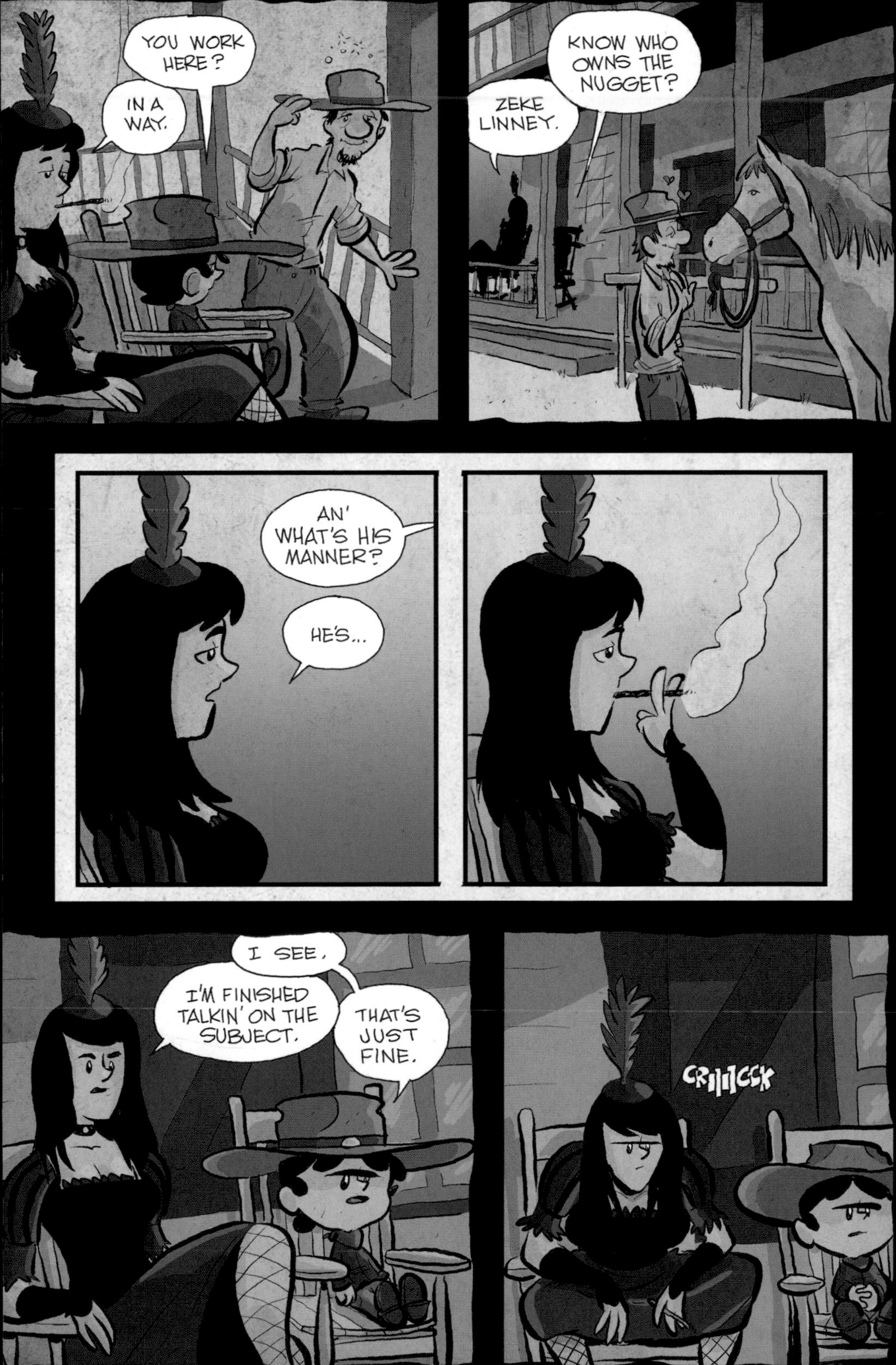
YOU WORK HERE?
IN A WAY.
KNOW WHO OWNS THE NUGGET?
ZEKE LINNEY.
AN' WHAT'S HIS MANNER?
HE'S...
I'M FINISHED TALKIN' ON THE SUBJECT.
I SEE.
THAT'S JUST FINE.
CRIIICCK

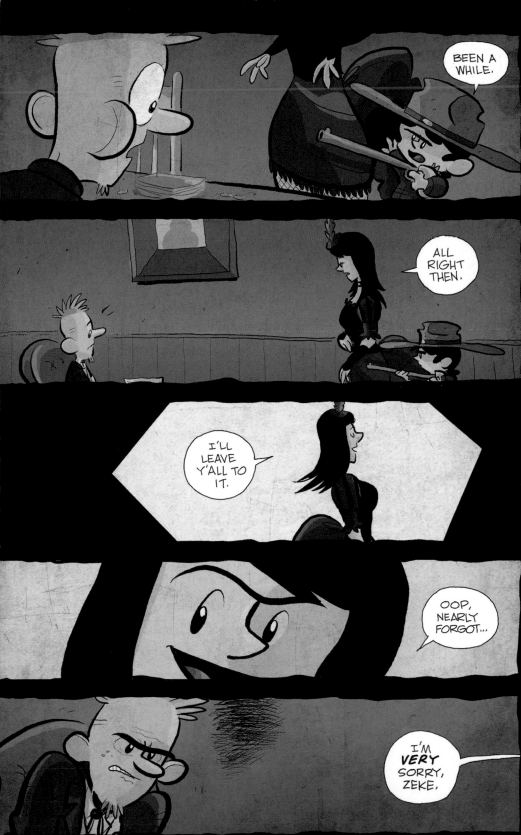

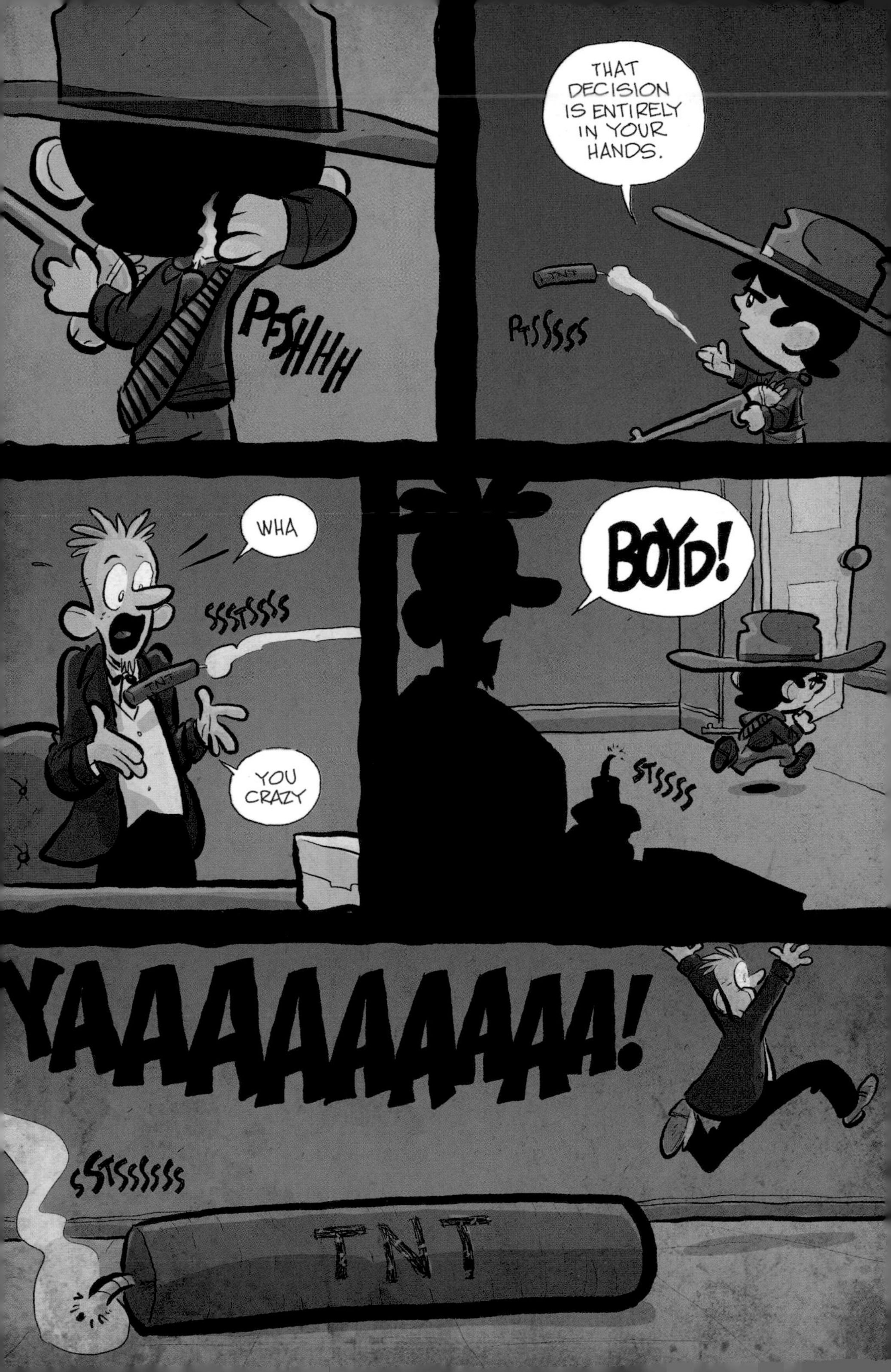
PFSHHHH
THAT DECISION IS ENTIRELY IN YOUR HANDS.
PFSSSSS
TNT
WHA
SSSTSSSS
YOU CRAZY
BOYD!
STSSSS
YAAAAAAAAA!
SSTSSSSSS
TNT

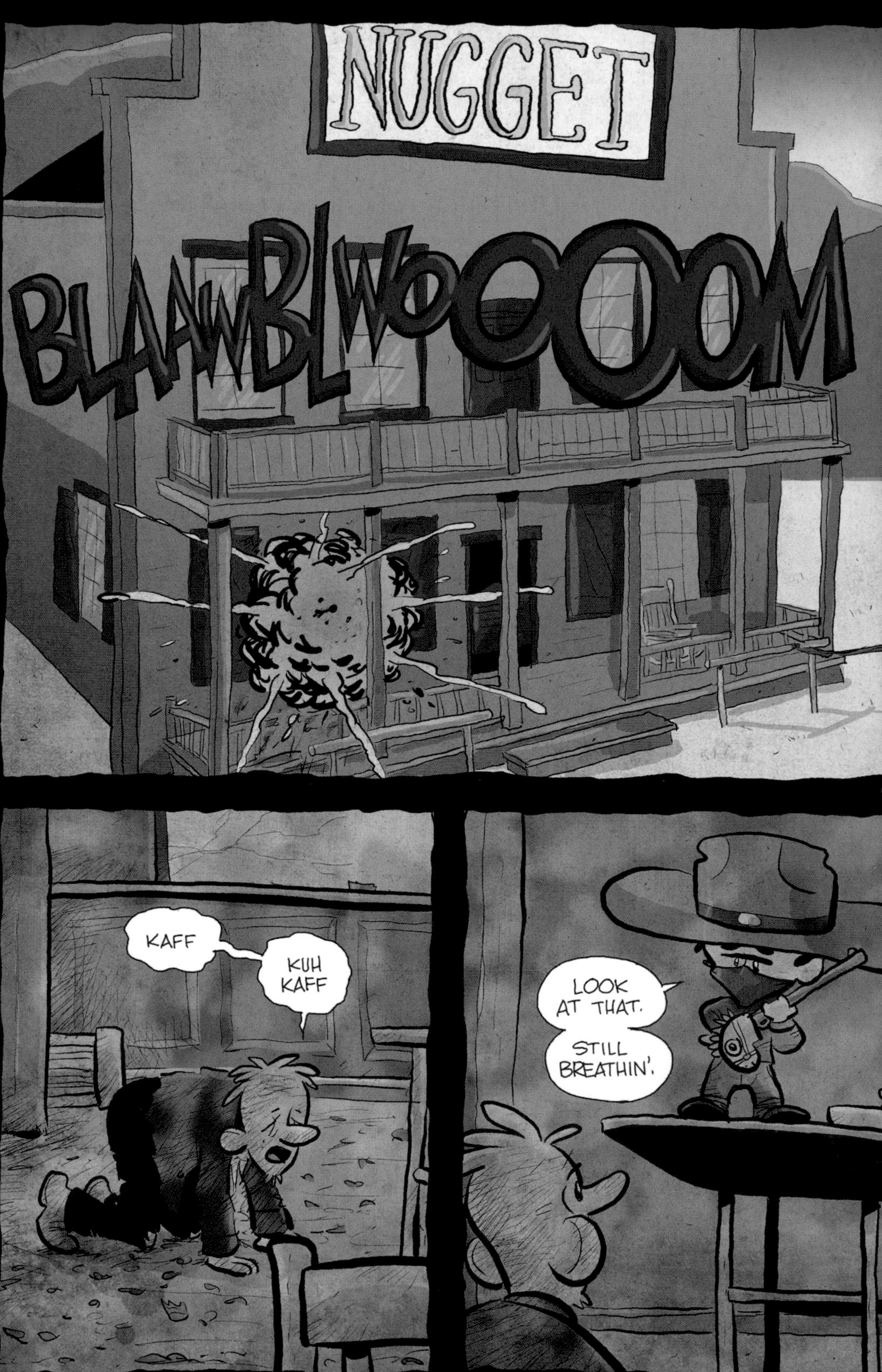
NUGGET
BLAAWBLWOOOOM
KAFF
KUH KAFF
LOOK AT THAT.
STILL BREATHIN'.

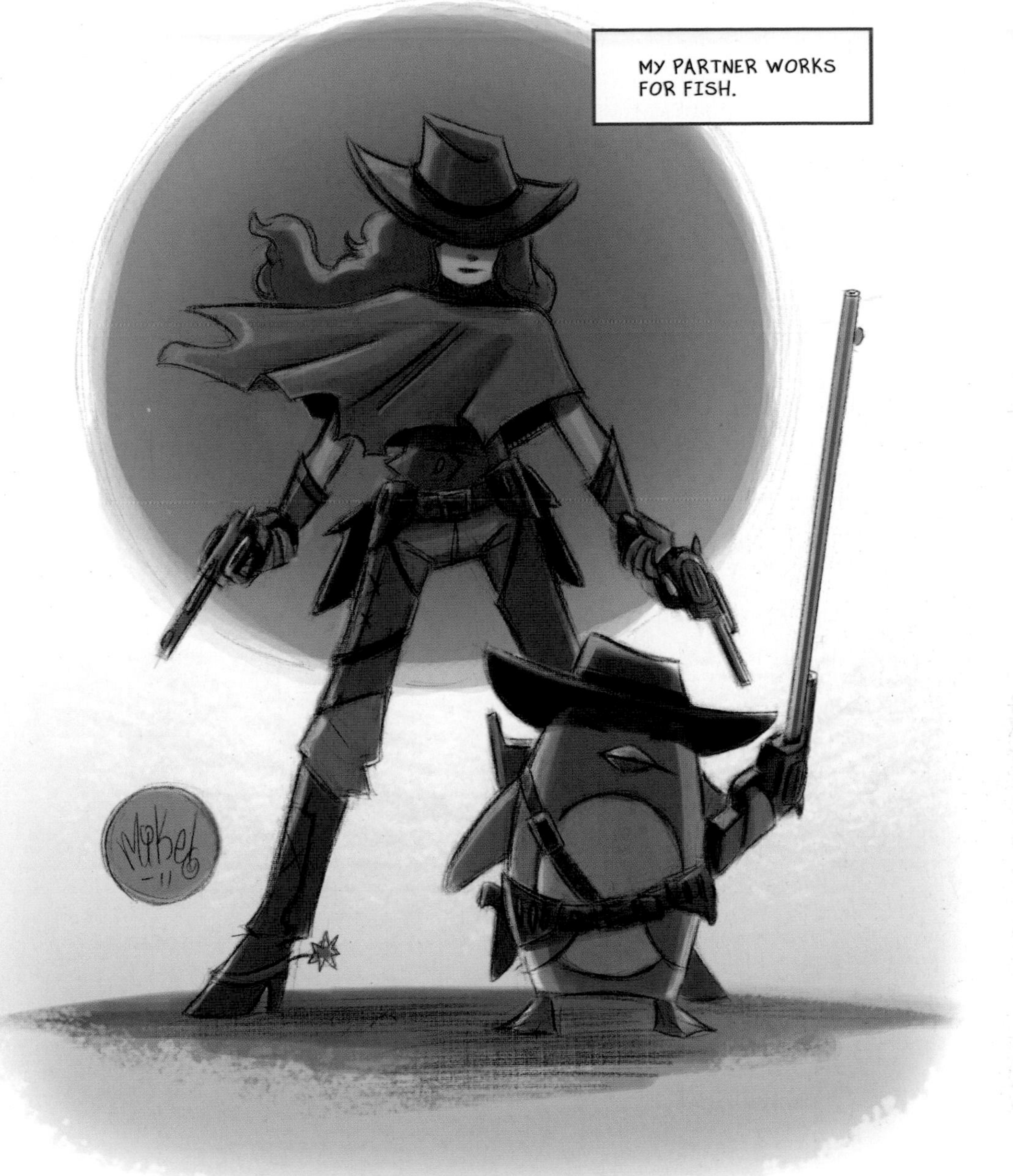
MY PARTNER WORKS FOR FISH.

A PENGUIN NEVER MISSES

STORY AND ART BY
MIKE MAIHACK

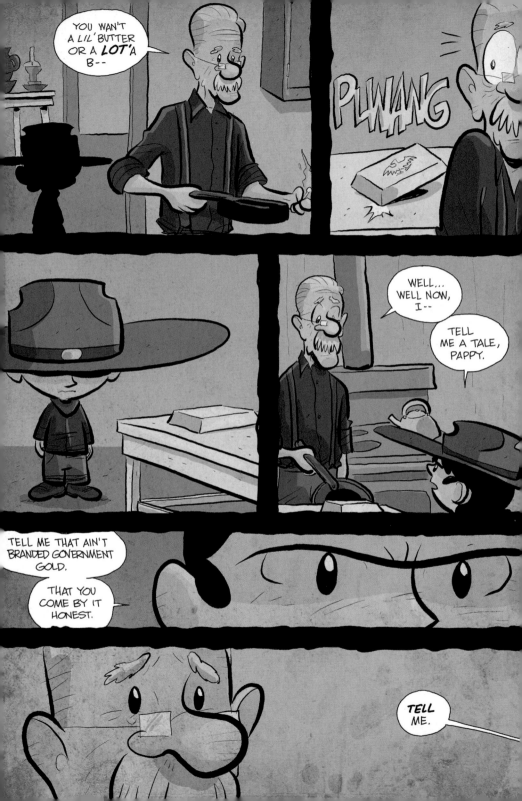

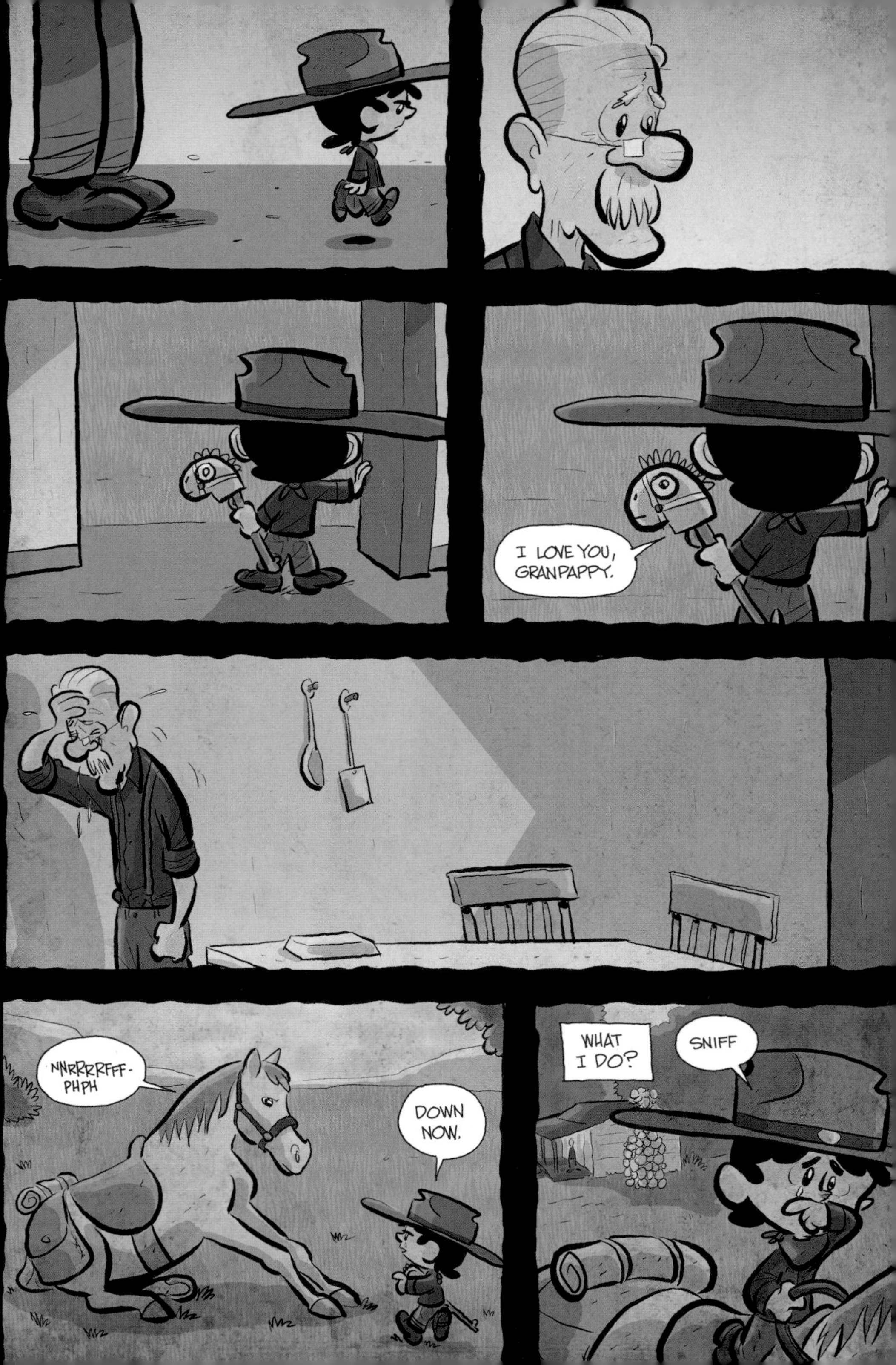
I LOVE YOU, GRANPAPPY.
NNRRRRFFF-PHPH
DOWN NOW.
WHAT I DO?
SNIFF

NATE COSBY

was born in Memphis and raised in Mississippi. He was an editor at Marvel Entertainment for six years, overseeing acclaimed series including the Harvey Award-winning Thor The Mighty Avenger, the Eisner Award-winning Wonderful Wizard of Oz and Marvelous Land of Oz, as well as X-Men First Class, Spider-Man, Pride & Prejudice, Sense & Sensibility and many others. Nate's been a producer/writer for PBS' relaunched Electric Company, where he developed animated properties (such as Captain Cluck). He edited Immortals: Gods And Heroes and co-wrote/edited Jim Henson's The Storyteller for Archaia Entertainment, and currently writes Buddy Cops for Dark Horse Entertainment and Pigs with Ben McCool for Image Comics.
Follow Nate on Twitter: @NateCosBOOM.

CHRIS ELIOPOULOS

has been telling stories for as long as he can remember. He started in comics as a letterer working on more comics than he can count. (Mostly because he's bad at math) He's also written and drawn the Eisner and Harvey nominated Franklin Richards: Son of a Genius as well as writing the acclaimed series, Lockjaw and the Pet Avengers for Marvel Entertainment. He's also the author of the webcomic, Misery Loves Sherman. He's short and likes to stay home with his lovely wife, Audra, and their awesome sons Jeremy and Justin and he hates writing in the third person.
Follow Chris on Twitter: @ChrisEliopoulos.